AWAITING
HONESTY

AWAITING
HONESTY

M. MANASSAH

ShaBazz Enterprise Publishing

Contents

Acknowledgement

Dedicated: To all the girls and women in the world who have ever been through something.

I would like to thank my mother, Sarah, for believing in my writing ability, encouraging me to express myself and being my inspiration for starting and completing my first novel. Thank you to my sister, Rebekah, for offering continued support and feedback during my writing process. Thank you to my two childhood best friends, Ashlynn and LaToya for their continued support, and a special thank you to my editor, Denise, who is both blunt and lovely, it was a pleasure getting an unbiased opinion. Finally, I would like to give a special acknowledgement to my son, Malachi, and my daughter, Honesty. Honesty was in my womb when I began writing this story and in my arms when I completed it.

One

As I sat crossed legged on the floor getting my hair braided by Mama, I wondered to myself why Daddy wouldn't just let me wear my hair straight like Coco and Candy.

Mama would say, "That hair on their heads ain't hardly theirs."

I knew they wore a lot of makeup and bought their hair in bundles that they would have the local beautician sew in their heads, but they still looked nice to me.

Daddy had many girlfriends, but Coco and Candy were who my daddy called his "best girls." Coco was short and had smooth Hershey chocolate skin. She was nearly flat-chested, but she made up for having no breasts by having enough behind for two women. All her clothes fit tight on her petite frame. Even in her highest heels, she only reached about five feet. She was small with big hips and a big butt, but she had an even bigger personality. Coco talked a lot and popped her bubblegum when she wasn't biting it with her teeth and twisting it around her index finger. Mama hated that.

Candy on the other hand, had light caramel skin and hazel eyes. She was usually quiet; her facial expressions spoke for themselves. She rolled her eyes and made faces more than she spoke. Candy had bright fire-engine red hair that she kept straight down her back. She wore the front of her hair in a Chinese bang. Candy was tall and shapely like an hourglass. She always smelled sweet like the Tootsie lollipops she stuck between her plump, red painted lips.

As a child, I didn't see anything wrong with my father having so many "girlfriends." Mama referred to them as "working girls." They gave my daddy whatever cash they made for the week when they came to the house for a hot shower, or to change their clothes and get a plate of Mama's home cooked food.

My Mama could cook. She made all our meals from scratch. As a homemaker, she spent a lot of time in the kitchen. All the while, my baby brother, Junior, stayed glued to her hip as she ironed clothes, washed dishes and stirred the steaming pot on top of the stove.

Mama never wore makeup like Daddy's girlfriends. She had soft, smooth brown skin. Her complexion was nearly flawless except for the dark marks underneath her eyes from lack of sleep. Mama kept her hair pulled back in a messy bun at the nape of her neck and secured it with a scarf or handkerchief. She often wore loose fitting clothes and house shoes. She had lost all the weight she'd gained from having Junior, but she still wore the oversized house dresses and robes she'd worn while she was pregnant. I knew Mama was pretty; I just wondered if she knew it.

"Hold still," Mama warned as she parted my hair with a wide tooth comb.

"Ouch! It hurts."

"Girl, if you don't hold still, I'll give you something that hurts," Mama threatened, attempting again to get my part straight.

I hated to be scolded in front of Coco and Candy. My eyes filled with tears and I fought to keep them in. I didn't want them thinking I was a baby. My eyes began to burn from holding the tears back and Coco and Candy became a blur through my tear-filled gaze. Mama combed through my thick hair, forcing my eyes to betray me. Big salty tears rolled down my cheeks. I began to sob, mostly out of embarrassment.

"It hurts," I whimpered.

"Girl, if you don't sit still..." Mama began but was cut off by Coco.

"I don't know why you don't just perm that child's head," Coco said not waiting for a response before she went on. "You know, downtown at Betty's Beauty Salon they do the girls hair half price every Thursday." Coco paused to pop her bubble gum before adding, "Rita, if you want, I could get you an appointment for little Missy," Coco offered.

"Her name ain't Little Missy, it's Mia, and I ain't putting that mess in my daughter's hair," Mama shot back.

Coco put her hands on her hips, rolled her neck and started to respond when Daddy walked in the house. Coco and Candy got up from the table where they had been playing cards and stood up directing their eyes on the floor. Daddy rushed into the house oblivious to the scene he had almost witnessed.

Daddy spoke to Mama first, "Rita can't you open a window? It's hot as hell in here."

"Hi Daddy!" I said with a smile, wiping my tear stained cheeks.

"Hey baby!" he yelled back halfway down the hallway.

Daddy was a busy man, and he was always in a hurry. Coco rushed to clear the table and Candy went to open the windows without a word.

Once Daddy had gotten home, the house grew so quiet you could hear Junior snore from the other room. Mama managed to finish my hair and make Daddy's plate while he was in the shower and getting dressed. My hair was parted off in eight sections held by balled-ponytail holders at the top of my braids and barrettes at the bottom. Mama put two ribbon bows in front. My long braids fell a little past my shoulders and shined from the coconut grease Mama used to condition my hair. On my way back from putting the hair products underneath the bathroom sink, I lingered a few minutes in the mirror.

"Not too bad," I thought, but I was nearly ten years old and Mama insisted on ponytails and barrettes as if I were a 2-year-old! I rolled my eyes at my reflection wishing I looked more like Candy. My thoughts were interrupted when Candy rushed past me and sat on the toilet to pee. I hurried to leave the bathroom to give her some privacy.

As I was closing the door I heard Candy laugh and say, "It's okay, we both girls. We all got the same stuff."

On my way to the kitchen table, I could hear Daddy's voice. He didn't sound too happy. I decided to eavesdrop. He was in the den, and I could see Coco's small frame from the shadow on the wall. It looked as though she were pacing and trying to explain herself.

"This is unacceptable! You think I'm stupid?" Daddy yelled at her.

"No, I just..." Daddy drew back and slapped Coco across her face.

I saw that he had a wad of money in his hand when he drew back again. This time the blow caused Coco to lose her balance in her tall high heels, and she fell to the floor. My heart began to beat fast, and I started to back away from the door when I bumped into Mama.

"Girl, go on to the table and eat your dinner." I rushed off towards the kitchen, not wanting Mama to know I had been snooping.

"Alright Donald, let the girl up. She ain't gone be no good to you if she black and blue," I heard Mama in the distance nervously attempting to defend Coco. A few moments later Daddy joined me at the table.

"Hey, baby girl," he said with a smile and then began to bless the food. Candy was feeding Junior in his highchair when Mama came into the kitchen.

"Go on girls and get yourself something to eat," Mama said.

Coco entered the kitchen wearing dark sunshades. It looked as though she didn't have on any makeup, and her lip was swollen. Both of Daddy's girlfriends went to make their plates and then sat quietly at the table and ate their food without a word.

Two

I'd never felt ashamed of my family or our lifestyle until I went to 7th grade and started going to middle school. Candy's younger cousins went to the same school and were in the 8th grade. We didn't have any of the same classes except P.E. During that class, her cousins would tease me every day. They'd call me names and taunted me by singing that my daddy was a "P-I-M-P." Justine was the ringleader. She was tall and intimidated me with her green accusing eyes. She had wild light brown hair and a freckled face. She called me "the pimp's daughter" as if it were my name. Justine always walked around in a group of other kids, mostly her cousins. They were easy to identify because of their untamed manes and freckled faces. The constant teasing and name-calling went on for weeks, until one day during P.E., Justine threw the basketball at my back causing a sharp pain to shoot down my spine.

I turned around to see Justine's piercing green eyes staring at me with a smirk on her face.

"What's your problem?!" I yelled at her, forgetting I was afraid of her and her pack of wolves.

"Look y'all, the pimp's daughter is getting bold," she laughed.

"Why you always bullying me? It ain't my fault your cousin Candy is a ho!" I shot back at her.

Justine's smile faded from her face and one of her sidekicks came to her defense.

"What you say, little girl?" Her short, stocky friend asked getting up in my face.

"Watch out, Bella. I got this," Justine said as the other kids started to realize what was going on and began crowding around.

"My cousin ain't no ho! Your daddy is a dirt bag and your mama..."

I punched Justine in the face before she could finish her sentence. Before I knew it, my fist was pounding Justine's face like it was a punching bag.

I could hear all the kids cheering, "FIGHT! FIGHT! FIGHT!" I was sitting on Justine's stomach while she was laid out on the blacktop and I continued to wail on her. The rest of the fight was kind of a blur. I remember my P.E. shirt being torn by Justine's crew attempting to pull me off of her, but all my built-up rage had given me super strength. I kept punching Justine in the face until Coach Wilson yanked me out of the crowd. He literally picked me up and carried me all the way to the principal's office.

My heart was racing from the adrenaline rush, and I didn't fully realize what had happened until I sat in the principal's office holding a wet paper towel against my bloody knuckles.

I could hear ambulance sirens in the distance. Principal Ballard was a small, blonde haired white woman who spoke in a low, calm voice. She explained she would have to call the police to do a police report because of Justine's injuries, and that my mother was on her way to the school to pick me up. She kept asking me if I understood, but I never answered her. I just stared off into the distance.

I wanted to yell, "Justine tormented me for weeks with her minions!" I wanted them to understand she'd gotten what she deserved, but nothing came out. I just sat there for what felt like an eternity.

Mama showed up looking very stressed and concerned. Junior was on her hip, smiling and waving, completely unaware of the trouble I was in. Mama sent me to go sit in the car while she figured out what exactly was going on. When Mama finally came back to the car, she put my backpack on the back seat and then buckled Junior into his car seat. She got into the driver's seat, buckled her own seat belt and let out a deep sigh. Mama started the car and began to drive in complete silence. I was afraid to look over at her but too afraid not to. I decided against asking any questions. I would learn my fate soon enough. Nothing was going to prepare me for what was to come.

To my surprise, Mama pulled up to a diner near our home and told me to get Junior out of his seat. Once we got inside the restaurant, the young hostess greeted us with a bubbly smile.

"Hey, how y'all doin'? Thanks for joining us at John's Diner. Booth or table?" she asked.

"A booth is fine, and can I get a highchair for my baby?" Mama asked.

"Right this way y'all," she smiled leading us to a booth and grabbing a highchair for Junior on the way.

After we were seated with menus, Mama said, "Mia, I need you to pay attention." Mama let out a deep sigh before continuing. "A lot is going on Mia..."

I nervously interrupted, "Mama I ain't mean to hurt Justine, I was just defending myself."

"Hurt who?" Mama asked with a puzzled expression.

"Justine mama, you know my fight. I was just..."

"Girl, hush, I'm not talking about no school fight." Mama saw my confusion and explained, "Principal Ballard ain't gone put it on your record since it was a first offense, but she can't have you back at that school. So she's letting me voluntarily withdraw you from the district."

"What?!" I exclaimed.

Before Mama could respond, a heavyset woman wearing an apron appeared next to our table.

"Can I get y'all something to drink?" she asked ready to write on her small note pad.

"No!" Mama snapped. Then gave an apologetic smile and said, "I'll just have tea and sugar and she'll have a lemonade." Mama placed our food orders, while giving Junior his sippy cup from his diaper bag.

"Look," Mama began as soon as the waitress had walked away. "That school is the least of our worries," Mama paused and then said, "Your daddy was arrested today. He got picked up by the police this morning right after you left for school." I sat in shock.

"He's being held without bail; there's a whole lotta charges." Mama went on, "Pimping and pandering, possession of a firearm…" Mama's voice trailed off. "I can't begin to explain to you the charges. I just need you to understand that things are about to change."

The waitress appeared with our drinks and set our burgers and french fries in front of us. This explained Mama's weird behavior, and the diner, Mama had never taken us to a diner before. She would say, "Don't make no sense to pay for a meal I can prepare at home that would taste twice as good."

I watched Mama stirring her tea and noticed how puffy her eyes were, probably from crying. I imagined my daddy in jail and had to fight back tears of my own. Junior began to bang his cup on the table, pulling me from my thoughts. Mama was still talking. During our meal at the diner, Mama explained we would have to move from our house and that the police had frozen all the money in the bank accounts until Daddy was released. She said there was an ongoing investigation, and she had to spend almost all the cash Daddy had stashed away for a lawyer. My head began to spin. I had no appetite for the meal in front of me.

To think that I had thought my school yard fight was the worst part of my day! When we left the diner, Mama drove to a small motel. She'd packed our suitcases in the trunk. We spent the night in a small, musty motel room that smelled like stale cigarettes. Everyday Mama would go out early in the morning to look for a job, and I was left in the motel room to watch Junior. The small T.V. in the room only had four channels that showed a clear picture, and to make matters worse,

Junior would cry when he woke up and noticed Mama was gone.

I carried Junior on my hip to the nearest convenience store to get him some candy as a bribe and to get out of that small room. I was happy to find out the store had a cosmetic aisle. From then on, every time I went to get Junior candy, I would wait until the cashier was busy helping a customer. Then, I'd take a lipstick or eyeshadow and tuck it inside Juniors diaper bag. I'd pay for the candy and rush back to the room and stash the makeup away so mama wouldn't find it.

In my backpack, I had a green pencil case. It had a mesh front and a zipper down the side. I emptied the pens and pencils inside the top drawer on the nightstand. I put my stolen cosmetics inside the pencil case and tucked it away at the bottom of my backpack. By the end of the week, my pencil case could hardly zip. I had false eyelashes, nail polish, foundation, a variety of eye shadows, eyeliners, and lipsticks.

After nine days of living in that small room, eating from the vending machine during the day and fast food at night, Mama came in with a big smile on her face and announced she'd found a place. Junior was clapping and jumping up and down, but I doubted he even understood any of what Mama was saying. Mama rushed around the room collecting our things, mumbling to herself and thanking God all at the same time.

Three

We lived downtown in a one bedroom apartment for a year before it felt normal. Mama was working two jobs. I was taking a home school program so I could watch Junior while Mama worked as a chambermaid during the day at the Clifton Inn and as a waitress at night at Ben's Burgers. Right after we'd moved in, a towing company took Mama's car away. The white, beer bellied man seemed unaffected by Mama's pleading to allow her to keep the car.

"It's all I have, Sir. I have to get to work," Mama pleaded. "Look, I have kids. I can't just be stranded. Please!" Mama begged.

The man refused to unhook Mama's car and once again waved his court ordered papers in her face.

"Ma'am, I'm just doing my job. Sorry I can't help you," he said matter of fact like, as he finished hooking up the car to be towed. Mama became frantic.

"Mister, please! I just paid that car payment! What am I supposed to do?!"

The man became impatient with Mama and snapped,

"Look lady, I don't know what to tell you. This car is registered to a Mr. Sampson and the court ordered the repossession of this vehicle, so if you don't mind."

He closed the driver door in Mama's face and started his engine. Mama began to beat on the door with her fist while she held Junior tightly with her other arm. He must have sensed Mama's panic because he began to cry as Mama chased the tow truck that pulled our car down the street and out of sight.

I sat on the front steps of our building watching along with the nosey neighbors who were getting a free show. It was embarrassing to say the least.

That night Mama said, "Mia, if you don't take nothing else from this experience, I hope you learn this," she paused as though she was about to say something profound. "You can't depend on nobody but yourself. They took everything I had because it was all in your daddy's name." Mama muttered something underneath her breath and then said, "That man ain't never drove that car! It was mine! He drove his Cadillac, and I had the Honda since we bought it. But child, the only thing that matters is who signs the papers!" She said bitterly. "Girl, when you get grown, don't you be no fool. You get everything in your name. You can't leave nothing to chance." I listened to Mama rant and rave that night for hours while we unpacked our boxes.

We had a routine, and it worked for us. I enjoyed the freedom of spending most of the day without Mama's supervision. I began doing my own makeup every morning once Mama left for work, and I had it down. Since Mama was always so busy, she even let me manage my own hair. I kept it brushed up into a high ponytail, feeling real grown up as I gelled down my baby hairs in front with a toothbrush, the way I'd seen Coco do to her hair when I was younger.

My daddy's girlfriends were my inspiration for my everyday look. I wore bright red nail polish on my fingernails, just like Candy. I even kept a lollipop tucked in the top of my ponytail so I could take it out and eat it on the front steps when I was feeling cute. However, I didn't get my clothes together until I met Sasha.

She was a light skinned girl with dimples that lived on our block. Sasha was sixteen when we met. She dropped out of school the year before, because she had a daughter. Even though Sasha was two years older than me, we were about the same height and wore the same size. Everybody called her Shorty.

Every morning she would strut passed our apartment building pushing her daughter in her stroller. Sasha wore short shorts and had her t-shirt tied up in the back, so all her curves were on full display. One day when she was making her way down the street, she stopped by our steps.

"Hey girl, your son sho is cute."

I noticed she was smiling at Junior as I bounced him on my lap.

"I ain't one to judge girl, cause Lord knows I can't, but you look so young to..."

"He ain't mine," I cut her off. "I mean this is my little brother, Junior, and I'm Mia," I introduced myself.

"Oh, well he is so adorable. We should have play dates so Tati and him can play," she said as she motioned toward her daughter. "I'm Sasha, but everyone calls me Shorty," she said with her dimpled smile. Ever since that day, we were thick as thieves.

Sasha lived with her grandmother, Grandma Trudy. She was a dark-skinned woman who usually wore a housedress and slippers. Her grey hair was spun tightly in pink rollers. Whenever I came over, she was cooking something and watching her "stories." That's what she called the dramatic soap operas that she was addicted to. Grandma Trudy adored Junior. Every afternoon she'd feed him and Tati before rocking them to sleep and putting them down for their nap in Tati's bed. Junior became so used to Grandma Trudy, he'd cry when I told him it was time to leave.

Two years later Sasha, and I still hung out every day. We would leave the kids with Grandma Trudy and rush upstairs to get our outfits together. Sasha had so many clothes and heels; I envied her walk-in closet and vanity table full of makeup. Sasha loaned me a pair of short shorts and a midriff baring tank top.

When I looked at the top with reservations, Sasha said, "Mia, you gotta show off your cute tummy before you get marks from a baby." She was referring to her stretch marks she'd gotten while pregnant with Tati.

Once we got our outfits on and faces full of makeup, we'd strut down the block feeling cute. "Hey, Shorty," Donte said pulling Sasha in for a hug. He took the liberty of squeezing her butt with his large hands.

"Boy, stop!" Sasha giggled. All the boys on the block were always checking for Sasha. Donte was tall and chocolate and usually had his shirt off. He could flash his big white smile and make any girl swoon.

"Hey, Donte," I said bashfully.

"Hey, Mia. You know my boy, Coffee, wanna holla at you," Donte said still holding Sasha.   "Boy, please!" I said rolling my eyes.

"What you gone diss my boy? A'ight then, that's messed up." Donte said smirking.

"If he wanna talk to me, he better do it himself. He don't need no messenger boy," I said sounding meaner than I intended.

"Why your girl stuck up?" Donte asked Sasha.

"Who Mia? She just playing. She know she would love to holla at Coffee," Sasha said attempting to defend me. I sucked my teeth and rolled my eyes.

As if on cue, Coffee rounded the corner in his black Chevy Impala. He had dark tint on the windows, but everybody knew it was Coffee's car from the music we could hear blasting from his stereo system halfway down the block. My heart began to beat fast and my palms were sweating. I put my hands on my hips and pretended not to notice Coffee pulling up beside us. The passenger window rolled down and Coffee motioned, "What's up," to Donte with an upward nod of his head.

There was a white girl sitting in his passenger seat looking shy, as Sasha and I glared at her. I rolled my eyes and directed my attention towards Sasha.

"Girl, you ready? I gotta go pick up Junior," I said sounding annoyed.

Coffee lowered his blasting music.

"Hey, Mia, you want a ride? I can give you a lift back to

your spot," he offered. Coffee's deep raspy voice took me by surprise.

I played it cool and said, "No thanks, looks like you already got your car full and I'm not no backseat girl." I shot back.

"Come on, Coffee, let's go,"the white girl whined.

Coffee smiled and said "Okay, see you later, Mia."

The tinted window rolled up. My heart began to beat normal as he pulled away. That was the longest conversation we'd had and it was over so fast. Why did that white girl have to be in his car, I thought as I pulled my eyes away from him and realized Donte and Sasha were both smirking at me.

"What?" I asked turning to walk back to Grandma Trudy's. I could hear Donte laughing.

"Man! Coffee in the doghouse now! You don't mess with mean ol' Mia," Donte joked.

"Girl, wait up!" Sasha called rushing to walk beside me.

"Coffee has his nerve," I said once Donte was out of earshot.

"Oh please, Mia. Coffee is checking for you!" Sasha squealed.

That night as I washed the dishes, my mind was a thousand miles away wondering what Coffee was doing and who he was with. I couldn't get the image of him out of my head, but the memory of that girl riding shotgun in his car didn't sit well with me. Coffee had a reputation in the neighborhood. He was one of the few guys that had his own car, and he stayed fresh from his fitted caps down to his clean Nikes. He was one of the major hustlers on this side of town, but he wasn't in the neighborhood often. Sometimes it'd be weeks before I saw his car on the block. His mysterious nature is what I found most appealing. Coffee had a presence about him; he wasn't loud like Donte, but he sure got a lot of attention.

I was pulled from my daydream by Mama's voice.

"Girl, do you hear me talking to you?" she asked with a frown on her face.

"Yeah, Mama," I lied.

"I'm on my way to work. I have to leave a little early so I don't miss my bus," Mama said while getting dressed. "I guess they changed the bus schedule. I was nearly thirty minutes late for my shift last night," Mama complained.

"But like I was saying, I want you to finish that homework packet tonight. Junior's already down for the night," Mama said putting on her stud earrings.

"Okay Mama," I answered, so she knew I was listening.

"And take off that damn red nail polish" she ordered before kissing my cheek and heading to the door wearing her waitress dress and tic-tac looking shoes.

"Bye Mama" I said once I heard her close the door.

I rushed to get the cordless phone to call Sasha. She'd called during dinner but Mama didn't allow me to take phone calls during dinnertime.

All I heard Sasha say was, "I have a message for you, from you know who," before Mama interrupted. I told Sasha I would have to call her back. I knew her message was from Coffee by the excitement in her voice.

Sasha's phone rang a few times and then went to voicemail, "Hey y'all it's Shorty. Leave me a message and if I want, I'll call you back." I hung up and tried again.

I wondered what Coffee wanted to tell me, as I finished the dishes and started my math homework.

The phone rang and I answered it as quick as I could "Hello? Sasha?" I said.

"Hey, Mia, I hope you don't mind. I got your number from Shorty." his deep raspy voice said through the phone. My heart began to beat so fast it sounded like a drum in my ears.

"Hello?" he said.

"Who is this?" I asked trying to calm my nerves.

He laughed and then answered, "It's Coffee. Look I was trying to get a message to you by my boy, but he told me you would rather me do it myself." I smiled knowing Donte delivered my message.

"I can respect that, so do you have some time to talk?"

"Umm...Sure...What's up?" I asked with a smile on my face.

"Come outside. I'm in front of your steps." Coffee stated matter of fact like.

"Give me a minute. I'll be down in a few."

I rushed in my room and changed out of my sweatpants and t-shirt and put on a short, grey sweater dress and black boots. I brushed my hair into a neat ponytail and put on strawberry lip-gloss. I sprayed my wrists with perfume and looked at my reflection in the mirror thinking that it would have to do. I peeked at Junior asleep, sprawled across the bed before making my way to the door and rushing downstairs to meet up with Coffee.

His black Chevy was parked right in front as promised, and I stood at the bottom of the steps with my arms crossed in front of my chest. Coffee leaned over and opened the passenger door from the driver's seat. I rolled my eyes and climbed inside.

"Is this how you open a lady's door?" I asked with an attitude.

"Oh, excuse me your highness!" Coffee said jokingly.

"I'm babysitting so I can't stay long," I admitted feeling like a kid.

"That's cool. I just wanted to see you, and you know apologize if I offended you earlier."

"If you're dating that white girl that's your own business," I said sounding jealous.

"Who Katie? Naw, she just needed a ride and since we use to go to high school together, I gave her lift."

I shrugged and pretended not to care but I was happy he'd felt the need to explain himself.

"Look, Mia, I wanna get to know you. You know, chill," Coffee said as he leaned in to kiss me on my strawberry glossed lips. I felt like I melted into his seat as his cologne filled my nostrils and his hand began to massage my thigh as we kissed. My head was spinning and I let out a moan as Coffee's hand moved up my thigh and inside my panties.

"Coffee, we should stop" I said as I started to feel less in control of my own body.

Coffee moved back into his seat and said, "Look, Mia, I want to talk to you, and I had to do a lot of begging to get Shorty to give me your home phone number." I rolled my eyes imagining Sasha enjoying every minute of Coffee's attention. Coffee went on, "So while I was out, I got you something."

He opened the glove compartment and handed me a box that was too big to be jewelry.

I anxiously opened the box, "A cell phone!" I exclaimed, immediately feeling embarrassed that

I sounded so excited.

Coffee smiled and said, "I'm glad you like it. I took the liberty of storing my number inside. I hope you don't mind me calling you sometime." He looked at me with questioning eyes.

"Sure, but I gotta go. I have my little brother upstairs," I explained while reaching for the door handle.

Coffee leaned in again and kissed me on the lips. I felt my heart flutter and I rushed upstairs to the apartment feeling as though I were floating.

Four

"So how did you get the name, Coffee?" I asked looking at Coffee through a haze of smoke. He coughed, passing me the small white joint we were smoking.

"My granny named me. She raised me. My mama wasn't ready for no baby; she was only 15 years old at the time, and my Pops split before she even peed on the stick."

"But why Coffee? I mean, I like your name, but it's different," I said taking the joint from Coffee and putting it out in the ashtray.

"Well, it ain't that different. My mama wanted to name me Black," Coffee laughed. "Believe it or not she's light skinned, her and my granny. But I guess I got my color from my pops. My granny said she'd never seen such a black baby," Coffee smirked as though he were reminiscing.

"You know why I like smoking with you?" I asked with a smile.

"Cause I got good weed?"

"No, for real," I laughed, feeling my high. "It's because when you smoke, you're so open. I could listen to you talk for hours and not get bored."

"Not tonight, babe. We don't got hours," Coffee said as he

got up from the motel bed, reaching for his basketball shorts on the floor.

"I gotta get back to the money," he said pulling his white t-shirt over his head.

I sat up wrapping the sheet around my chest.

"Yeah, the money," I mumbled rolling my eyes.

"Don't look so down, girl. If a man can't make money, he can't provide," Coffee reminded me, leaning in and kissing my lips. Coffee always knew what to say to get on my good side.

We'd been talking and texting every day since the night he bought me the cell phone. Coffee's hustle often kept him out of town for a few weeks here and there, but with our cell phones we were able to keep in touch. I felt I knew everything about Coffee, except how exactly he made his money. I knew he "moved product" as he called it, referring to drugs, and at times he would have pounds of marijuana in zip-lock bags boxed up and ready to transport out of town. However, I didn't know the specifics. Whenever I questioned him about his hustle he would say, "The less you know the better." I didn't like being kept out of the loop, but he was adamant about not involving me in his business transactions. That was the only part of his life he kept private. The rest was an open-book.

Coffee had opened my eyes to a whole new world. He'd given me wads of money and let me spend it however I wanted. Once he spent nearly two thousand dollars on a purse I'd picked out at the mall. When the saleswoman told him the total, he didn't even flinch. I noticed her eyes become wide with greed when he took out his money roll. I started to become very accustomed to the lifestyle provided for me, but even with all the money and gifts we didn't become official until he took me upstate to visit my daddy.

Our relationship had gotten serious after we were having a casual conversation one day, and I mentioned that my father was incarcerated. Coffee suggested we take a road trip so I could visit him.

I kept my plans a secret from Mama because I didn't want her to put a damper on my day or ruin my excitement. Even after all these years, Mama was still angry at my father for leaving us. That Tuesday couldn't come soon enough. I waited at the bottom of the steps on a cloudy October morning anxiously waiting to see a black Chevy come around the corner. I'd already walked Junior to school, and Sasha agreed to walk him to Grandma Trudy's after school got out. I waited in the cold, holding the bag of snacks I'd prepared for our road trip.

I was surprised to see Coffee pull up in a rental car. He hopped out dressed in an olive-green bomber jacket, grey Levi's and olive green Nikes with his fresh white t-shirt matching the white check mark on his shoes. I smiled from ear to ear, so excited about our trip. Coffee opened my door with an exaggerated wave of his hand as though he were a chauffeur.

"You're too crazy," I said before climbing into the passenger seat.

"What happened to your car?" I asked as Coffee opened the sunroof.

"I didn't wanna put too many miles on my baby, so I got this for the day."

He said we had a long ride ahead of us, so I should

sit back and get comfortable. My mind was racing with antic-ipation, and I couldn't relax.

"You're quiet," Coffee said glancing over at me.

"Just thinking," I said being pulled from my thoughts.

"Yeah I figured, cause you're sure not talking," he joked.

"Sorry, I'm just nervous you know. I haven't been to see my daddy since he got locked up and my mama ain't want me writing or sending pictures."

"Damn that's cold," Coffee said shaking his head. "He couldn't even get a letter."

"I guess my Mama have her reasons," I said feeling the need to defend her.

"When I called the visitation hotline, I had to enter all this information just to be put on the list."

"It's just protocol. As long as they gave you a day and time for your visit, you straight," Coffee said trying to calm my nerves.

"I got something to help you relax," Coffee said knowingly.

He reached under the seat and handed me a lunchbox. In-side were rolled joints, a small ziplock bag of weed, a lighter, and a pack of rolling papers.

"When's the first time you blazed?" Coffee asked smirking.

"Last year, when I was chillin with Sasha, We spent the rest of the night laughing like hyenas and Sasha lost her cell phone, or so we thought. After looking for it for hours, she found it. In her purse!" I said laughing at the memory of that night.

"Y'all a trip." Coffee said shaking his head.

"Light up." He said with a smile.

Coffee and I smoked three joints and ate all the snacks I'd packed by the time we reached the prison.

We stopped at a gas station when we were close so I could freshen up. I bought eye drops, bubblegum and car air freshener. Coffee laughed at me as I sprayed the car down using almost the entire bottle of freshener.

Once I had been checked in and searched by a female guard, I was lead to the visitation room. To my surprise, we weren't going to be separated by a glass window, speaking to each other through a telephone like I'd imagined. I was sitting at a small metal table connected to a bench seat that was bolted to the ground. I watched as several inmates came into the visiting room and sat across from their loved ones, keeping their hands flat on top of the table as the guards looked on observing their visit. I tried not to stare as I watched the inmates greet their visitors with excitement.

Coffee waited in the car for me. He said if I were his daughter, he wouldn't want to see me with no guy, no matter how fresh he was. I started to get butterflies in my stomach as I waited while looking around the room.

"Mia." I looked up and saw Daddy dressed in an orange jumpsuit.

I stood up and wrapped my arms around his waist, resting my ear against his chest. I could hear his heart beating fast. I reluctantly pulled away and sat across from him at the small table. Daddy looked as though he'd aged ten years. He had a thick beard and mustache and creases of frown marks on his forehead. Even so, my daddy was still handsome the way I remembered him when I were a little girl.

I started to speak, but instead I began to cry.

"Now, Mia, I know you didn't come all the way up here to cry." Daddy said wiping my tears from my cheeks. "How's your mama? How's Junior?"

I took a deep breath.

"Come on, Mia, we only got a little time and a lot of catching up to do," Daddy reasoned.

I didn't know what was wrong with me. I'd waited years to be face to face with my daddy again, and now that I was, my tears wouldn't stop coming.

"Junior won the 2nd grade spelling bee," I managed to say.

"My boy! That's good," Daddy said proudly.

"Mama still always working, but she's good." I said sniffing.

"She's a strong woman, your mother." Daddy paused and then finished,

"You look good, Mia. It look like you got a good head on your shoulders. You just have to apply yourself, Mia. My baby girl all grown up," Daddy said as though he were talking to himself.

"Get your diploma, Baby Girl. Don't get lost in these streets," Daddy lectured.

"I'm not saying you can't live your life, but stay focused. Recreational weed here and there is alright, but don't make it a habit."

My eyes got wide and I sat up straight on the hard bench seat.

"I was just nervous to come today..." I began to explain feeling guilty.

"Mia, I want you to tell your mama that I love her, and she'll always be my number one girl," Daddy said.

"We vowed 'til death do us part and I stand by that promise I made before God," Daddy said in a serious tone.

"Mama don't know I came up here, Daddy," I confessed looking down at my hands and

avoiding his eye contact.

"I know your mama is upset about things, but give her my message. Can you do that, Baby Girl?" Daddy asked lifting my chin with his knuckles.

"So who's this boy you're seeing?" Daddy asked knowingly.

"I...umm...what?" I stammered.

A loud voice came over the intercom. "Visiting hours are now over. Please return to your designated areas at this time." The announcement continued asking all the visitors to leave the visiting room as the guards began to interrupt people's visits, telling them "Times up!" in a harsh tone.

"I just got here!" I complained.

"I know, Baby Girl, but there will never be enough time for me to explain to you how much I love you," Daddy said standing up.

"Take care of yourself, Mia. Make good decisions and kiss your mama and Junior for me."

I rushed to give my daddy a hug as a guard approached.

"Alright, time to go," he said rudely.

Daddy kissed me on my forehead and walked out of the visiting area.

Five

Mama had recently started seeing this guy she'd met at the restaurant. He was fat, short and bald. I couldn't stand him. He had the most annoying laugh and he drove a hooptie. He was just a pathetic excuse for a man, but he loved my mama, and she loved her some James. She'd come home with flowers and talk on the phone with my Auntie Glen for hours about what sweet things James did or said. It was always James this and James that. She would even invite him over! Mama would be giggling like a schoolgirl when she and James were in the kitchen making dinner together. I liked to see my Mama happy, but it was enough to make a person sick.

It took me a week to find the courage to tell Mama I had went upstate and saw Daddy, and he'd wanted her to know he still loved her and honored their wedding vows. Mama practically laughed in my face.

"He don't have no choice but to honor our vows. He's in prison! Your daddy is a lot of things, but he's no homosexual."

"Mama, I'm serious. He wanted me to tell you that you're still his number one girl and he know you're still angry with him, but he still loves you," I said trying to talk Mama into loving Daddy again.

"Child, please, I'm his 'number one,' but he had a number

two, three, four, five, and six, all standing on the corners for him. When they locked those whores up, they all sang like canaries. Now he rotting in jail, and I'm his 'number one'? Humph!" Mama said shaking her head.

I got upset listening to Mama bash my daddy.

"Well at least he cares about his wedding vows you both took before God, Mama. You're not even divorced and you're dating that midget of a man!" I yelled.

"Girl, watch your mouth when you talk to me! You think you're so grown up, but you're still naïve. Your daddy ain't respect a vow a day in his life, and don't you bring God into this.

The Lord said, 'Thou shall not kill,' and he killed that whore with his bare hands!" Mama shouted and then realized she'd said more than she intended.

I grabbed my purse and ran out of the apartment, leaving the door and Mama's mouth wide open. I ran all the way to Sasha's house with the cold night wind stinging my nose and ears. When Grandma Trudy opened the door, she looked at me with wide eyes.

"Child, where is your coat and shoes?"

I looked down at my ankle socks as I walked into the warm, aroma-filled house. I hadn't even noticed I didn't have any shoes on, but now the soles of my feet began to ache from the cold, hard cement sidewalk.

Grandma Trudy put a blanket around my shoulders and said, "Sasha went to the store for milk, but sit on down and get warm."

I sank into the couch thinking about what Mama had said. Was it true? Was it an accident? How could she keep that from me for so many years? My head was spinning with questions.

By the time Sasha had gotten home, I had already ate, helped Grandma Trudy with the dishes and went to lay down in Sasha's queen size bed. I was falling asleep when I heard her open the door and tiptoe inside the room attempting to be as quiet as possible.

When she flipped on the lights she gasped.

"Jesus! Mia, I ain't know you were here."

I sat up shielding my eyes from the bright light.

"Me and Mama had a fight."

"Well, you can crash," Sasha said kicking off her heels and unzipping her dress.

"I called you, but your phone was going straight to voicemail."

"Oh, my phone battery died a long time ago," Sasha said matter of fact like.

"Grandma Trudy told me you went to get milk hours ago," I pried.

"Yeah, that's what I told her," Sasha said washing off her caked-on makeup.

"What you and Rita fighting about now? I swear, Mia, your mama is so uptight. I don't know how you do it."

"You know how I told you my daddy was in prison for a gun charge? Well that wasn't the whole story. He also got booked on pimping and pandering charges,"

Sasha looked at me surprised as she brushed her teeth.

"My mama told me tonight he was actually locked up for murdering a whore." I said still not ready to believe it.

Sasha stopped brushing her teeth mid-brush.

"Oh, my God!" she said with a mouth full of toothpaste, going into her bathroom to spit. I heard the water running and then Sasha returned drying her hands on a towel.

"Girl, you sure have a weird way of thinking about things. Maybe she was trying to protect you from the truth. I mean a blind man could see how much you adore your daddy."

"She said he killed her with his bare hands," I said thinking about Mama's words.

"The pimp game is brutal," Sasha said knowingly.

We both sat in silence, Sasha looked as though she were thinking about something complex.

"Well, my mama didn't have to keep that from me for all these years just to throw it in my face!"

"Girl, you're freaking me out! Did you tell Coffee about all of this?"

"No, Coffee's out of town for the weekend and besides, I don't want to stress him with my family drama."

"He might understand your problems better than you think."

"Thanks, Dr. Phil," I said laughing.

"So, where you been all night?" I pried.

"You know me. I'm not no house rat. I been in the streets!" Sasha bragged.

"I gotta go kiss Tati goodnight. I'll be back."

"Tati been asleep for hours," I informed her.

"Yeah, but I kiss her every night while she's asleep. I think it gives her good dreams," Sasha said on her way down the hallway to Tati's room.

"Whatever you say, Sasha" I mumbled as I rolled over drifting off to sleep.

I woke up to see Tati standing next to the bed smiling at me with her two front teeth missing.

"Gram said come eat," she said.

I groaned, closing my eyes. Tati opened my eyelid with two of her pudgy fingers.

"Are you woke?" she asked.

I pulled myself up from the bed and walked to the bathroom.

"Mama, wake up! Gram said come eat." I heard Tati saying, moving on to harass Sasha.

When I came out of the bathroom, Sasha was still in bed. She was holding the pillow over her head, and Tati had given up and gone back downstairs.

I grabbed my purse and started to look for my shoes when I realized I'd come over without any. I borrowed a pair of Sasha's boots and a pull-over hoodie before heading downstairs. I could smell sausage and eggs from the kitchen.

"Good morning, Grandma Trudy. I'll see you later," I said as I rushed to the front door.

"Ain't you gone eat?" I heard Grandma Trudy ask from inside the kitchen.

On my way back to our apartment, I could see James's bucket of a car parked in front of our steps.

"Oh great," I thought sarcastically.

I'd left my key so I had to knock. Junior opened the door holding a box of cereal.

"Mama mad at you," Junior said before I could even come inside.

"Where she at?"

"In the kitchen," Junior said before putting his hand inside the cereal box and stuffing a fist full of dry cereal in his mouth.

James came out of the kitchen holding a coffee mug. I rolled my eyes and headed toward my room.

"Good morning to you too, Mia," James said laughing his annoying laugh.

"Mia is that you?" I heard Mama call from the kitchen.

I went inside my room and slammed the door. I got my cell phone out and noticed I had a new text message from Coffee. While I was texting him back, Mama opened the door.

"Mia, I hope you're not being rude to our company," Mama said from the doorway.

"What company?" I shot back.

"He practically lives here." I said as I continued to text on my phone.

"Mia, we need to talk," Mama said in a hushed voice as she entered the room.

"Oh, so now we need to talk? After you kept the truth from me for years?"

"Mia I'm not going to have you disrespecting me. There are things you don't know about your father, because you are a child. You don't need to know everything, Mia."

"I am not a child. I'll be 18 next month! So stop trying to hide the truth from me."

"Okay Mia, you're right," Mama said to my surprise. "The truth is I've already filed paperwork to get out of this marriage with your father." I looked up from my phone.

"I'm waiting for his signature and the divorce will be final." Mama took a deep breath.

"The truth is James and I are getting married. I haven't worn my engagement ring because I was waiting for the right time to tell you, but since you're so grown up and desperate for the truth there it is!" Mama walked out and closed the door.

I laid back on the bed feeling defeated.

Six

A few weeks later, I got a letter in the mail stating I'd successfully completed the 230 required academic units to receive my high school diploma. My heart was pounding as I read the letter. I was so relieved that all the homework packets and tests had paid off. Not only was I graduating, but I was graduating months ahead of my class! I had great news, but no one to share it with. Me and Mama's relationship had been strained ever since she told me her "truth." That night, she announced her engagement, and I decided to move out. Mama looked as though she could care less.

Mama came by Grandma Trudy's to drop off my mail and she brought Junior to play with Tati, but she didn't stay long. She gushed about her stupid wedding plans with Grandma Trudy and she beamed as she showed off her engagement ring. I just rolled my eyes from where I was standing at the top of the stairs and went back into Sasha's room. When Mama left, I went down stairs.

"I'm not going to get in your business, because it's not my place. But you only get one mama!" Grandma Trudy said handing me my mail and going back to the kitchen.

Now, I'd gotten great news and I doubted Mama even cared.

Coffee was out of town on business and Sasha just wouldn't understand. I decided to walk over to Mama's apartment and drop the letter off. Even if she didn't care, at least she'd know I'd accomplished something. When I knocked James opened the door smiling. The sight of him annoyed me. I rolled my eyes and handed him the letter.

"Please give this to my mama," I said as I turned and walked away.

When Coffee called, I told him about my good news. He sounded thrilled

He said with my birthday coming up, this was even more reason to celebrate.

"Come with me this weekend."

"Where we going?" I asked excitedly.

"Las Vegas. My Moms is having something out there that I gotta show up to, and while we're in the city we can celebrate," Coffee paused and then added, "We have a lot to celebrate, with you graduating, and I got somewhat of a promotion myself,"

"What kinda promotion?"

"Mia, you know I don't talk business over the phone. Just know we're going to have a good time."

"Sounds like fun. You know I love a road trip."

"Speaking of road trips, have you been keeping in touch with your Pops?"

"Yeah," I lied. The truth was I hadn't gotten over what Mama had told me, but I didn't want Coffee to know about my daddy's dark past.

"So, when are we leaving?" I asked changing the subject.

As I packed my bags for the weekend, Sasha was getting

ready for her own night of fun. She was wearing a tight red tube top dress and 6-inch red stiletto heels. She sat at her vanity table doing her makeup in front of her mirror.

"Too bad you can't come to Vegas with us," I said as I held up different dresses trying to decide what outfits to take.

"Girl, please! I'm not trying to be third wheeling the happy couple. Besides, I have to get out in these streets," Sasha said powdering her face with foundation.

"You're addicted to the streets," I teased.

"Well, all of us ain't got a man paying our way," Sasha said bitterly.

"What's that supposed to mean?" I snapped.

Sasha ignored my question and emptied a small vial of white powder onto her vanity table. I cringed as I watched her snort a line of white powder in her nose.

"I didn't know you did crack," I said with disgust.

"It ain't crack; its cocaine," Sasha corrected, "And there's a lot you don't know," Sasha said rubbing the white residue from her nose with her fingers.

"I have to earn my money, Mia. I ain't got no mama taking care of me or no man giving me money. I work for mine," she
said proudly.

"So you're a prostitute now?" I asked feeling betrayed.

"You make it sound so bad. I like to think of myself as a 'working girl.' That's what they call us in the streets," Sasha laughed, going back to doing her makeup.

"You ain't gotta do that, Sasha. Don't Grandma Trudy help you?"

Sasha rolled her eyes.

"Gram's social security check can't fund my lifestyle. She

can barely make ends meet. I got a child, Mia. I don't just work for me I'm doing this for my baby girl, and if you can't understand that..."

She was cut off by my cell phone ringing. It was Coffee.

"Hey babe, I'll be out in a minute. Oh, you're running late? That's cool. I'm running a little behind too. Okay, see you soon." I hung up the phone and noticed Sasha watching me.

"Was that Coffee?"

"Yeah, he's on his way," I said putting the last of my outfits in my suitcase.

"How long you say y'all gone be out of town?"

"Just 'til Sunday night"

"You ever think about joining the business?" Sasha asked brushing her long black weave.

"You gotta be kidding me," I said in disbelief.

"Well, excuse me 'Miss Goody Two Shoes,' but didn't you tell me your daddy was a pimp?"

I grabbed my bags and left the room without saying another word to Sasha.

"Tell Coffee I said, 'Hi!'" I heard her yell as I dragged my bags down the stairs.

Coffee booked us a 5-star luxury suite at a hotel on the Las Vegas Strip. Our room looked like something out of a movie. We had a king size bed, a Jacuzzi in the room and a balcony with a view that overlooked the city. It was breathtaking. I tried to clear my head so I could fully appreciate our weekend, but I kept thinking about Sasha and wondering how I didn't notice she was a part of the business. Just when you thought you knew someone they always showed you who they really were.

"We're supposed to be celebrating. Why you looking so sad?" Coffee asked opening a bottle of the expensive wine that had chilled on ice.

I forced a smile.

"I think I need to prepare you for tomorrow," Coffee said handing me a glass of wine, and then pouring one for himself.

"Why? What's tomorrow?"

"It's my mom's commitment ceremony."

"Commitment ceremony?" I asked puzzled.

"Yeah, like a wedding I guess. Her and her long term girlfriend are getting married," he said searching my face for disapproval.

I nearly choked on my wine.

"You okay?"

I coughed, catching my breath.

"I'm fine. I'm sorry. You never told me your mom was..." I stopped short not knowing what words to use.

"She's gay, Mia," Coffee laughed.

"You can say it. Hell, tomorrow you're gonna see it." We both laughed.

"So you're cool with it?" I asked.

"Yeah, it's cool. My Moms is happy and Step-Moms is cool. Last Christmas, Moms and Tori came down, and man, you shoulda seen my family flip. Granny just can't accept it," Coffee said drinking his glass of wine in one gulp.

"Is your granny coming to the ceremony tomorrow?"

"Naw, she don't approve. She said she's gonna stay home

and pray for Moms, and maybe she'll find a good Christian man," We both laughed.

"Well, I'm glad you invited me, and you trust me enough to share this experience with you."

"Of course I trust you, Mia. I love you." Coffee said using the "L word" for the first time.

"I love you too," I said feeling butterflies in my stomach.

I downed the rest of my wine and stood up, wrapping my arms around Coffee's shoulders. He picked me up and I wrapped my legs around his waist as he carried me to the king size bed.

After Coffee made love to me, he sat at the end of the bed rolling a joint. I slid out of bed and headed for the shower. We had plans to go downstairs to the casino. It was nearly 2 a.m., but Coffee said Las Vegas didn't sleep, so neither could we. As I stepped out of the steamy shower and wrapped a large terrycloth towel around me, I could hear Coffee in the other room raising his voice. He was on the phone. I'd never heard Coffee yell before. He always spoke in a calm tone and when he was upset, he lowered his voice, which somehow seemed more threatening.

I moved toward the bathroom door trying to make out what he was saying. I could only catch pieces of the conversation. I wondered who he could be talking to so late at night.

"If she's a problem, take care of it." I heard Coffee say in a low voice, as I came out of the bathroom tying my robe. Coffee noticed me in the doorway and went outside on the balcony to finish his conversation. When he returned, he was noticeably upset. I was sitting on the bed rubbing lotion on my legs.

"It was just business," Coffee explained as he noticed my questioning eyes locked on him. When he saw I wasn't satisfied with that answer he said, "Look Mia, there's just parts of my hustle you can't know about. It's for your own good."

"Did that call have something to do with your promotion?" I asked. Coffee looked puzzled. "You said you had somewhat of a promotion of your own when we were on the phone the other day. I know you said you didn't want to talk business over the phone, but I'm right here, and you said you trusted me. So tell me what got you so upset?"

Coffee sat on the bed and lit his joint before responding.

"Mia, I need you to trust me when I tell you I don't want you involved in my hustle. I appreciate you being concerned. I can tell you care about my well-being, but you gotta stop questioning me."

Coffee took a long drag from his joint and exhaled smoke before he continued.

"I've recently started covering new territory, and I have somewhat of a new staff. A few people have tried to test me which is fine. It's to be expected. I have to make an example out of those people, so the others will know I'm not one to play with. You have to command respect. When you start giving second chances, people lose respect for you. It's bigger than the offense. It's about principle. This is a brutal game, and if it's not played correctly, game over." Coffee said handing me the joint.

So much of what Coffee said reminded me of my Daddy's own philosophy, I remembered him saying similar things when I were a child. Coffee's phone rang and he got up.

"I gotta take this," he said as he went outside to the balcony closing the sliding glass door behind him.

I decided I wouldn't ask any more questions about his line of work and just enjoy our weekend together. Coffee and I were rarely able to spend quality time, so I wanted to enjoy every minute of it. I put the joint out in the ashtray feeling relaxed and ready to party. I dressed in a light blue romper with silver flats. I accessorized with silver bangles and big hoop earrings. My hair was swept up into a topknot and I was putting the finishing touches on my makeup when Coffee came out of the bathroom wearing a long sleeve, crisp collared shirt and denim jeans.

"You're beautiful. Are you ready to go?" Coffee asked holding the door open for me.

I smiled grabbing my purse and fake I.D.

We strolled through the casino holding hands, drinking and laughing. When Coffee spotted a roulette table, we stopped so he could play, and I stood beside him drinking and cheering him on. I noticed his cell phone vibrating at the edge of the table. It was so loud in the casino you couldn't hear it ring. The screen lit up and displayed, "1 missed call: Shorty." I looked in my purse to check my cell phone, but I didn't have any missed calls. Coffee's cell phone began to ring again, but this time he grabbed it.

"I gotta take this," he said as he walked away from the table.

I stood with my hands on my hips as Coffee returned, putting his phone in his pocket.

"Business." he said as he noticed my attitude. I rolled my eyes and headed back to our hotel room.

To my surprise, Coffee didn't chase behind me. He just watched me, as I stormed away. What kind of game was he playing? And Sasha! Who did she think she was calling my man's cell phone and at this hour!

In the elevator, I considered calling Sasha to ask her what her deal was, but I decided against it. I wasn't about to give her the satisfaction of hearing me in a jealous rage. The more I thought about it, the angrier I became and the alcohol in my system didn't make it any better.

I heard Coffee stumble into the room as the sun was coming up. I'd been tossing and turning for hours, unable to clear my mind. When I rolled over to face him, I was shocked to see Coffee standing in the room with one white girl under each arm as they supported his weight. Coffee drunkenly staggered toward the bathroom with the help of the two blondes.

"Get out! Both of you, get the hell out of my room!" I screamed.

Both blondes were wearing tight, short dresses, heavy makeup, and high heels. They were clearly drunk.

"What's her problem?" one of the girls asked looking confused.

"Chill, Mia," Coffee managed to say. "Shhh..." he shushed me while stumbling towards the sink.

I was furious. I yanked one of the blondes by her hair and pushed her out into the hallway.

The other one got the hint and ran through the open door and down the hallway. I turned to see Coffee hovering over the sink as though he were going to puke.

"Coffee, what the hell is wrong with you? First you're getting late night calls from my best friend, and now you're bringing hookers to our hotel room," I said accusingly, crossing my arms in front of my chest.

Coffee began splashing water on his face from the bathroom faucet. He stumbled towards the bed and before I could say anything else, he was sprawled out snoring. I turned off the running water.

While Coffee was sleeping, I managed to pull his cell phone from his pocket. I was happy to see his phone wasn't locked, and I was able to access his recent calls. I took the phone and went into the bathroom, locking the door behind me. I sat on the cold tile floor and began to scroll through his recent calls. Almost all the contacts were stored under nicknames that I didn't recognize. I noticed I was stored in his phone as 'wifey.' When I saw Shorty appear multiple times, it peeked my curiosity. My heart began to race as I opened his text messages. I opened the text message conversation from Shorty.

Hey Coffee, or should I say daddy? Lol. I heard U runnin things since Mouse is out of the picture.

945 p.m.

Call me

11:26 p.m.

So u need my help?

4:08 p.m.

Can I trust u Shorty?

4:12 p.m.

Come on now, you really gonna ask me that?
4:12 p.m.

Just collect for me and I'll make sure you're properly compensated.

11:25 p.m.

When you coming home? The street is hot. 5-0 everywhere!
2:18 a.m.

Coffee can you talk?
11:37 p.m.
Call me

2:32 a.m.

Sum of the girl's money is short, but Diamond said she'll have it for u Thursday
12:34 a.m.

Shorty u kno if u play wit my money u playin wit yo life!!!

3:15 a.m.

Come on Coffee, u kno me
3:16 a.m

Leo is handlin all business til I'm back in town.
10:17 a.m.

I felt like my heart stopped when I heard Coffee groaning from the other room. I exited the text message screen and opened the bathroom door. I was relieved to hear Coffee still snoring. I put his phone on the dresser and tried to make sense of everything I'd read in Coffee's phone. It all began to sink in. Coffee was a pimp!

Seven

The reception was beautiful. After the commitment ceremony, all the guests were led next door to a formal ballroom. There were huge crystal chandeliers hanging from the high ceilings. The room held about fifty round tables covered with ivory and pink tablecloths. Every table had a tall vase centerpiece that held long stem flowers. Pink and white rose petals were beautifully scattered around the floor and on top of the tables.

I was surprised to find out the wedding was a star-studded event. Tori worked as a crew member at a major film production company. There were over 300 guests and I recognized many of them from movies and television. It took me awhile to feel comfortable in a room full of famous actors and actresses, and at first I couldn't stop staring.

As I relaxed, my eyes moved round the room trying to take everything in and save it all to my memory.

I would have to rely on my memories alone since all the guests were required to surrender their cell phones and cameras before they were escorted inside. I was taken aback by the protocol that everyone else seemed so familiar with. We were even required to sign a confidentiality agreement!

The reception was so over the top. They had spared no expense. There was a live band on one side of the room and a full orchestra on the other. The ballroom was so big that the two could have been being playing at the same time and the crowd wouldn't have noticed. The guests were served appetizers and wine, as we waited for the couple to be announced.

Whenever there was an empty wine glass a waiter or waitress would appear to refill it. We were offered a choice of white or red wine. I noticed there was a fully stocked bar but they weren't serving drinks yet.

The room was loud with laughter and chattering as the guests talked amongst themselves.

"Are you alright?" Coffee asked taking my hand.

I was pulled from my thoughts, but I smiled.

"Fine," I said.

"You look beautiful," Coffee complimented me.

I'd worn a short black cocktail dress and black high heels. My hair was in a low, side ponytail. I'd accessorized with my favorite small diamond stud earrings. I was glad I had decided to wear this outfit because everybody knows you can't go wrong in a little black dress. It worked for any occasion and I hadn't expected this at all.

"Thanks," I said as a tall, thin, dark skinned woman welcomed all the guests using a microphone.

She asked all the guests to stand as she welcomed the newly committed couple, "Mrs. and Mrs. Bradley."

The guests clapped and cheered as both women entered the room linked arm and arm, holding a bouquet of white and pink roses. Loud music blasted from the sound system as party streamers fell from the high ceilings.

"Let the celebration begin!" the speaker said before cueing the staff.

A line of waiters poured through the doors, holding trays of food, splitting off from their single filed line as they began serving each table. Coffee's mom and Tori took their seat at a long table that looked as though it had been prepared for royalty.

"Wow!" I exclaimed at the extravagance of the reception.

After dinner, the dance floor was opened up for dancing. Coffee took my hand and led me through the crowd to meet his mom and her partner. Coffee's mom was a light-skinned petite woman with a big smile. She and Tori were wearing matching business skirts paired with a matching blazer. His mom wore the suit in ivory and Tori's was light pink. They were talking and laughing like best friends when Coffee interrupted.

"Hey, Moms, meet Mia," Coffee said holding my hand.

"Congratulations, Mrs. Bradley," I said.

"Oh, call me Natalie. And this is Tori," She said introducing her partner. Tori was a white woman with short, brown hair. She stood about five inches taller than Natalie.

"Nice to meet you," she said.

Coffee gave his mother a hug, kissing her on the cheek and then hugged and kissed Tori as well. I watched as Coffee interacted with his mother and I could feel the love he had for her. Watching Coffee tower over her, standing six feet tall with his broad muscular shoulders showing visibly through his tuxedo. It was hard to imagine that this tiny woman gave birth to Coffee.

I don't know what I was expecting, but Natalie and Tori's

relationship seemed so normal. Coffee danced with his mother for the "Mother-Son dance" and then he danced with Tori. Coffee was his mother's only child and Tori didn't have any children. As the photography bulbs flashed, I was jealous that I wouldn't be able to get any pictures of my own since my cell phone had been confiscated at the door. Coffee pulled me into pose with him for pictures, and then we took some with his mom and Tori.

I was so tired by the end of the night; I'd already ditched my heels underneath the table when Coffee pulled me up for another dance. The music had slowed down and we were both tipsy. We slow danced as I draped my arms over Coffee's shoulders and he held me by my lower waist.

"Do you trust me?" Coffee's deep, raspy voice whispered in my ear.

"Mmhmm," I said wondering what was on his mind.

After I'd snooped through Coffee's cell phone the night before, I'd slid into bed and had fallen asleep, only to be woken up a few hours later to Coffee's bulging manhood against my lower back. Of course, we'd had great make up sex, but we hadn't actually made up. There wasn't any dialogue, and without a proper conversation, I just couldn't quite forgive Coffee for his behavior, not to mention his secret life.

"You ready to get out of here?" Coffee asked.

"Yeah, I'm having fun, but I'm so tired."

I grabbed my shoes and went to the restroom to freshen up as Coffee said his goodbyes. I was happy to be headed back to the hotel with hopes of having a real conversation with Coffee.

After our cell phones were returned to us from our assigned storage box, we waited outside in the cold air for a valet to bring the car around. I turned on my cell phone and saw ten missed calls, all from Mama. She'd also left two voicemails. Coffee draped his suit coat around my shoulders as I began to tremble from the cold breeze.

"Thanks, Babe," I said as I put the phone to my ear to hear Mama's first message.

"Mia, its Mama. Call me as soon as you get this."

I deleted the message and selected the next message Mama left an hour later.

"Mia, I need to know you're okay! It's about Sasha. They found that poor girl dead in an alley! And I'm worried sick. Please call me back when you get this. I love you."

My heart felt as though it had stopped beating, I was in shock. I couldn't breathe; it felt as though I were having a panic attack. I tried to gasp for air, but the last thing I remember was my cell phone slipping from my fingers and everything went black.

I woke up to the sound of a beeping monitor and a sharp pain in my hand. My throat was so dry.

"Where am I?"

The beeping persisted and a tall, heavyset woman dressed in scrubs entered the room.

"Oh, look who's awake," she said as though she were talking to a young child.

"I'm Diane and I'll be your nurse tonight."

I forced my eyes open wider so I could look around the room.

"Where am I?" I asked panicking.

"Oh, you're in good hands, Hun. You're at the Las Vegas

Medical Center. It looks like you took a pretty nasty fall and you passed out. Dr. Brim only had to put a few stitches though. You'll be fine," she said smiling.

I touched my forehead and felt a small gauze bandage secured with tape.

"Where's Coffee?" I asked.

"Are you thirsty? You have a water pitcher beside your bed, and you're getting plenty of fluids through your I.V. line," she informed me.

I looked down at my right hand and noticed I had an I.V. that was connected to the beeping monitor.

"I have to get out of here," I said remembering Mama's voicemails.

"Oh sweetie, you were very dehydrated. You'll have to finish your I.V. and then I can see if the doctor wants to discharge you home."

She stopped the monitor from beeping and started to leave the room.

"Wait! I need to call my mother."

"You can dial out using the bedside phone, just press 9 first then the area code."

"Thank you," I said before she'd left the room.

"Your call-light's on the left, push it if you need anything," she said closing the door behind her.

"Mia!" Mama said with panic in her voice. "Girl where have you been?!"

"Mama, what happened to Sasha?" I asked as I began to cry. Mama ignored my question.

"Mia, I'm just so glad you're safe. Lord, you worried me half to death. I tried to report you missing and the police said

I couldn't even make a report until it had been over 48 hours, and I would have to come back in the morning..."

"Mama!" I yelled cutting her off.

"Where is Sasha?!"

"Baby, I'm so sorry about your friend," Mama said in a low voice.

My tears began to roll down my face and fall onto my hospital gown.

"Mama, what happened to Sasha?"

"Mia, the police found her body in the alley over there by Crane Street. She was badly beaten. It took hours for them to identify her. Trudy identified her body at the coroner's office by her tattoos." Mama paused as I sobbed uncontrollably.

"She was just in the wrong part of town. There wasn't anything that anyone could do. I'm sorry, Mia. She was so young."

I hung up the phone and cried for hours. The nurse gave me morphine in my I.V. when she saw me crying, thinking that my tears were from physical pain. After she'd injected the strong pain medication into my I.V. line, I fell into a deep sleep. When I woke up the next morning, I saw flowers and a Get Well Soon balloon next to the phone by my bedside. I rolled over and saw Coffee sitting in a chair against the wall. He stood up when he saw that I was awake and walked towards me looking concerned.

"Get out!" I said coldly.

"Mia," Coffee said with a puzzled expression.

"Don't you touch me!" I warned, as Coffee attempted to hold my hand.

"This is all your fault!" I said as my tears returned.

"You're the reason my best friend is dead!" I accused, raising my voice.

Coffee went and shut the door before saying anything.

"Mia what are you talking about?" he asked in a hushed voice.

"I know you're a pimp, Coffee, and I know Sasha was working for you!"

He listened with a straight face.

I went on, "You were talking all that shit about commanding respect and teaching people a lesson! Did you have Sasha killed?" I asked with fire in my eyes.

"Lower your voice!"

"You threatened her! You told her she was playing with her life if she didn't have your money!"

"Mia..."

"I should call the police and tell them everything!" I threatened, picking up the bedside telephone. Coffee snatched the telephone and threw it on the floor.

"Mia! You need to calm down," Coffee said holding both my wrist.

"You're hurting me!"

"Okay, I know you're upset about your friend, and if I could take your hurt away I would, Mia, but there ain't a damn thing I can do about it," Coffee said letting my wrist go.

"I trusted Shorty with a project, and she was stealing. She was disloyal."

I laid back against the pillows unable to believe what I was hearing.

"If I could have prevented the hit and spared her life, I would have but she left me no choice." I began to cry.

"I know she was your best friend, Mia, but she just couldn't be trusted."

"She has a little girl," I said through sobs.

"Who's gonna kiss her little girl every night while she's asleep?" I asked thinking of Tati's toothless smile.

A nurse entered the room, and her smile faded as she saw my tears. She looked questioningly at Coffee, and then back at me.

"You alright, Hun?" She asked with a southern accent, looking at me with concern.

"How soon can she get out of here?" Coffee asked.

"Well, if you're feelin' better, the Doctor will release you by this afternoon," she said as she removed the I.V. from my hand and covered it with gauze and secured it with tape.

"Just put a little pressure on that, and it'll stop the bleed-ing."

I nodded, with tears still rolling down my face.

"Oh Hun, are you alright? How's your pain?" she asked as she lifted the bandage on my forehead.

I shrugged.

"Well, you're healing nicely. In a few weeks that scar won't even be noticeable with a little makeup on it," she smiled.

"Thank you," Coffee said, anxious for the nurse to leave. She looked at Coffee and then back at me.

"If there's anything you need, Hun, just push your call light." She rubbed my hand and then walked out of the room.

Coffee kneeled down on his knees beside my bed and held my hands.

"Mia, I'm sorry you're hurting. I will do whatever I have to, in order to mend your heart." Coffee said as he laid his head in my lap.

Eight

Sasha's funeral was held that following Sunday, which also happened to be my 18 birthday, I couldn't bring myself to go to the funeral service. I sat in the backseat of a cab watching the rain fall. I was thinking how fitting it was for a rainstorm considering the circumstance.

Last year, it had also rained on my birthday and Sasha convinced me the storm wasn't gonna stop our good time. We dressed in short, tight-fitting dresses and high heels and headed to the club. Sasha was fearless as she grabbed my hand and walked straight to the front of the line ignoring the fifty people she'd cut off that had been standing in the rain getting drenched. Sasha flashed her dimpled smile at the bouncer and whispered something in his ear, and he unclasped the black rope and let us inside. We didn't even have to show our fake I.D.'s. She was always the life of the party, and now that she was gone I didn't know who I was.

Maybe it was grief mixed with guilt that kept me from attending the service. I'd decided to keep my relationship with Coffee quiet and my mouth shut about what I knew. I rationalized my decision, because I had already lost my best friend, and I didn't see any purpose in also losing my boyfriend. Losing the love of my life wouldn't bring Sasha back, so as selfish as it may sound, I chose to keep what happiness I had left.

After a lot of thought, I decided to keep the promise I'd made to Grandma Trudy. I attended the memorial service that was being held at her house after the burial. I was dressed in a simple black dress and black pumps with my hair pulled back into a ponytail. I wore a big black church hat and a pair of dark sunshades. When I arrived to the house, I noticed most of the guests were Grandma Trudy's friends from her church and a few family members. None of Sasha's so called "friends" showed up. Grandma Trudy put out about a dozen framed pictures of Sasha that she'd taken through the years. I had never noticed how much Tati looked like Sasha, as I looked at a framed picture of Sasha holding her baby doll. She was about four years old in the photo and as cute as could be; smiling her dimpled smile at the camera.

"Mia, I'm so glad you could make it," Grandma Trudy said rubbing my arm.

"Hey, Grandma. How are you?"

"I'm staying strong. It's all I can do," she said forcing a smile.

I gave her a hug.

"Is there anything I can do? Can I help out with anything?"

"You can eat some of this food," Grandma Trudy joked. "I have so many dishes people have brought over. I don't know what to do with it all."

I smiled as I squeezed Grandma Trudy's hand.

"If there's anything I can do, Grandma, just call me. If you need me to help box up her room or sort through things..."

"Oh no, I couldn't bear to even go in there," Grandma Trudy sighed.

"I'm going to let Sister Healy from the church donate whatever she can to the shelter. You're welcome to grab anything you want." Grandma Trudy offered.

"Didn't you have some of your things in there?"

"Naw," I said with a wave of my hand.

"Nothing important. Where's Tati?" I asked, noticing I hadn't seen her.

"She's outside in the back, running and playing with her cousins. She's so young, it's not real to her yet," she said solemnly.

I bit my lip, fighting back tears.

"You know, she's about the same age Sasha was when I lost my Gloria," she said shaking her head.

"Sasha never told me what happened to her mother."

"They say it was an overdose and called it a suicide. But I still don't believe my baby would take her own life. I know it must have been an accident. She had so much to live for. So much life ahead of her."

I began to feel pangs of guilt as I watched Grandma Trudy fight back tears.

"I have to go," I said as I gave her another hug. "Please, call me if you need anything."

"Alright, Baby, you be careful and tell your mama I said thank you for the flowers."

I considered going to Mama's apartment but changed my mind. I just wanted to be alone. She'd left a voicemail that morning wishing me a happy birthday and Junior was in the background singing, "Happy Birthday to Miiiaaa!" The message made me smile until Mama passed the phone to James.

"Happy Birthday to the birthday girl!" he said.

It wasn't nothing happy about today, and I sure as hell wasn't a girl. I called a cab and went back to my hotel room. I had been living out of a hotel in town, since I'd gotten back from Las Vegas. I didn't feel like I belonged anywhere.

"Hey, Babe," I said as I opened the door and saw Coffee sitting on the bed counting money.

"Happy Birthday," he said without looking up.

"Aww...is all that for me?"

"Yeah, whatever you want," Coffee said playfully.

"You always give the best gifts."

"There's something I wanna talk to you about," Coffee said as he continued to shuffle through stacks of one hundred dollar bills. I sat on the bed in my bra and panties.

"What's up?" I asked lighting a cigarette.

"I've been thinking a lot about this, Mia, and the more I think about it, the more it makes sense."

Coffee put a band on the stack of bills, and began to count another stack.

"Thinking about what?" I asked impatiently.

"Mia, I want you to become a partner in the business."

"A partner?" I asked raising my voice.

"You expect me to be your drug mule? Or walk the streets for you?"

"No Mia, nothing like that," Coffee said smirking at the idea. "Mia, you're gonna be my wife. I wouldn't have you walking no streets. I just figured if you were gonna be my partner in life, why not be my partner in business? Besides, you've been asking for months for me to let you in on the details of my hustle. I thought you'd be happy,"

"What exactly does it mean to be a partner in the business?" I asked calming down.

"I bought a house out in Sundown Valley, and tomorrow I pick up the keys. I want us to move in together, and when I'm out of town, I need you to manage the house."

"What about the business part?" I asked with skepticism.

"Well, I figured we could manage the business out of the house."

I nodded as I considered Coffee's plan.

"So, we're gonna be running a brothel and a trap house out in the Valley?" I asked with apprehension.

"We're gonna be hustling and making money," Coffee corrected.

"I won't be there very often, because I have so many projects in different cities that I still have to overlook and maintain. I trust you to hold down the fort,"

"Alright 'Partner,' I'm in," I said putting my cigarette out.

"But there's just one stipulation."

"What's that?" Coffee asked.

"I want the house in my name." I said remembering Mama's advice.

* * * *

The house was a lot bigger than I expected. There were seven bedrooms and three bathrooms. The kitchen was big and spacious, with granite counter-tops, an island and all black appliances. The whole house had hardwood floors, except in the bedrooms. The Master bedroom was my favorite room in the house. It had his and hers walk-in closets and glass double doors that led to the balcony, which overlooked the backyards pool and Jacuzzi.

My toes sank into the soft, plush carpet, as I directed the movers where to put the king-sized bed, and where I wanted my vanity table set up. I was so tired, even though I didn't have to lift a finger. Coffee left me to dictate where everything would go. He'd hired a moving company that not only delivered, but assembled all the furniture. By noon, all of my indecisiveness had gone out the window, and I was quick to make decisions and tell them exactly what I wanted and expected.

Two months later, there were three "working girls" staying at the house, Brandy, Blondie, and Erica. Before they moved in, I'd decided I wasn't going to be their friend, but I was going to be a boss running a business. However, as I spent more and more time with them, the closer we became. Brandy was a tall brunette with green eyes. She was thin and she didn't have much of a shape. She kind of looked like your average girl-next-door compared to the other girls. I was surprised to see she usually had twice as many clients.

Blondie was a bleach blonde, with a dark orange spray tan and big fake boobs. She would play dumb and pretend to be more of a ditz than she actually was to come across as likeable. I found her to be pretty annoying. Erica was a short, curvy,

Puerto Rican girl that called all the other girls in the house "Chicas." She was loud and she complained a lot.

Coffee had strict rules that no clients were allowed in the house. All "guests" had to go to the pool house, or they went to a motel. By 7 p.m., the girls would be getting dressed and ready to go out to work. During the day, they'd go shopping or lounge around the house watching television, splashing in the Jacuzzi, sleeping, and eating.

At first, I wondered why the girls chose to live at the house, and not just work their corners and keep all their profit. I soon found out that having a pimp meant safety. They had a sense of security that the other woman on those corners didn't. Although I was new to the area, Coffee was very well-known. He had a reputation for being unforgiving and malicious if he were disrespected. Coffee had a lot of people working for him. Two of his guys would often keep surveillance on the house, keeping a close eye on the number of "guests" that came in and out of the pool house. Coffee's hustle was a lot bigger and organized than I'd imagined.

"Mia, my girl, Lexi, wanna come work for you," Blondie said as she chewed her bubblegum and twisted her blonde locks around her finger.

I rolled my eyes.

"Who doesn't?" I mumbled uninterested.

"She hasn't been in the business long but she's good at what she does, and she's loyal," she said before popping her gum.

"We don't need no more Chicas in this house. What we need is some testosterone," she suggested laughing.

"You know, not like just any guy but one of them fine men that play in the novellas."

"Excuse me, Erica, but I'm talking business, and you're talking television," Blondie said flipping her hair.

"You ain't gotta be rude, Bitch," Erica snapped.

"Look, 'Chica,' I'm not in the mood," Blondie said mocking Erica.

"Well, who made you a damn recruiter anyway? Nobody care about your damn friend," Erica said rolling her eyes.

"Enough!" I was growing annoyed with their arguing.

"Blondie, tell your friend she has to go through the process like everybody else. I have four working girls moving in this weekend so if she passes a seven day trial, I'll consider her."

"Damn, four more Chicas! I can hardly stand rooming with these two," Erica complained.

"Well, you can leave," I offered with a straight face.

"Oh, I didn't mean it like that, Mia, I was just saying." Erica retracted.

Brandy came downstairs wearing a red, long-sleeved, short fishnet dress with nothing underneath and a face full of makeup. She was carrying her heels and talking on her cell phone.

Blondie and Erica looked her over, rolling their eyes and sucking their teeth. Brandy hung up her phone ignoring the other girls' stares.

"I'm gonna head out a little early. I wanna be the first girl on the track tonight," she said putting on her heels.

"Sure," I said approvingly,

"Just tell Rick I said to drop you off."

"When are y'all leaving?" I asked turning my attention towards Blondie and Erica.

"Mia, it's only 6:15. I don't know where she gets off trying to make this a competition," Erica said giving Brandy a dirty look. Brandy laughed.

"I don't have any competition," she stated before turning on her heels and walking out.

I couldn't help laughing as the other girls were left with their mouths open.

"Somebody needa teach that girl a lesson," Blondie said bitterly.

"If you want to teach her a lesson, you need to beat her at her own game." I said.

Blondie looked confused.

"Bring in more money! Brandy is good at what she does. You can't knock her hustle," I defended Brandy. "Just step it up a little bit," I suggested.

Erica began to snicker.

"I wasn't only talking to Blondie," I said turning my attention to Erica.

"Both of you could learn a few things from Brandy,"

"Well if we're gonna have to go to work early, we might as well start drinking early!" Blondie suggested, getting a bottle of vodka from behind the bar. Erica jumped up to grab shot glasses.

I rolled my eyes feeling irritated. I hadn't been in the best mood lately with Coffee being out of town for nearly two weeks. With the constant bickering of his hookers, I was a little on edge. I had everything I'd asked for and then some, but deep down I still felt a void that even money couldn't fill.

My cell phone began to ring and I grabbed it and answered it quickly, hoping to hear Coffee's voice.

"Hello?"

"Hi, Mia, this Tati. Gram said I could call you and invite you to my birthday party on Saturday if you wanted to go."

I got up and walked outside to get away from Blondie and Erica's drunken laughter.

They'd turned on the stereo system and were dancing and having a good time.

"Are you gonna bring Junior?" Tati asked.

"I gotta work this weekend, Tati, but I will tell my mama to bring Junior."

"Ahhh man," Tati whined sounding disappointed.

"How old are you gonna be?"

"I'm gonna be 7," Tati said proudly. "And Gram said I can wear a princess crown like my friend had at her birthday party!"

"Well, what do you want for your birthday?" I asked.

"Ummm...," Tati said thinking it over.

"How about a Barbie doll?" I suggested

"I already got a Barbie doll, but she needs some new clothes," Tati said.

"Alright, Girl, don't start that begging," I heard Grandma Trudy warn in the background.

"I ain't," Tati protested.

"Tell Grams I said Hi, and I'll make sure your Barbie gets some new outfits," I assured her.

"Okay, bye, Mia."

"Bye, Tati," I said hanging up.

I felt guilty that I wouldn't be able to make it to her birthday party, but Coffee was depending on me to be here and manage the house this weekend when the new girls arrived.

I went online and ordered a Barbie doll dream house with matching Barbie Corvette and many different Barbie clothes. I also added four Barbie dolls to my online shopping cart and checked out. I was having it all shipped directly to Grandma Trudy's house. I paid for rush delivery to make sure Tati would receive her gifts in time for her birthday party.

When Coffee got home on Saturday morning, he was all business. He spent hours on the phone and hours meeting with his staff. When he finally came into our bedroom, he reminded me there would be four working girls moving in.

"Whatever," I mumbled flipping through the T.V. channels.

"What's the matter, Mia?" Coffee asked, sensing my attitude.

"I'm sick of being your business partner. I want to go back to being your girlfriend,"

"Mia, you know you're more than just my business partner. I love you," Coffee said with a smile.

"I know I've been busy lately, but I ain't forgot about you. In fact, I got something for you."

"What's that?" I asked putting my hand out.

"It won't fit in your palm. You gotta come with me," Coffee said taking me by my hand and leading me outside to the front yard.

"You've been doing a really good job holding down the house, so I want you to know how much I appreciate you," he said before turning me towards the driveway.

There was a light pink Bentley parked in the driveway with a huge white bow on top of the hood.

"Oh, my god!" I exclaimed as I stared in disbelief.

"And since I know how you love everything in your name, it's all yours," Coffee said handing me the keys and the pink slip.

I couldn't believe it. I hugged Coffee, wrapping my arms around his neck and kissing him passionately in front of all his staff and the working girls who watched enviously from the window.

Nine

After some much needed and well-overdue quality time with Coffee, I was in much better spirits. I cruised around the neighborhood driving my Bentley and feeling like a boss. I ran a few errands and loved the looks of admiration I received from onlookers. Coffee left to handle business, but promised he'd be back before midnight. I was looking forward to spending the night cuddled up with him and decided to stop by Secret Pleasures in the mall and get some new lingerie.

When I got back to the house I didn't even have time to put my bags down before Rick's Cadillac Escalade pulled up and dropped off the new girls, Trisha, Nikki, and the twins, Miracle and Destiny. Trish was a short, stocky brunette. She was cute but kind of chubby. As soon as she walked in the house she said, "Howdy y'all," with a cheerful southern drawl. Nikki was tall with red hair and freckles. She had a bad habit of biting on her nails and she looked as scared as a deer in headlights. Miracle and Destiny were almost identical, except Miracle had a birthmark on the right side of her cheek, and she was a little shorter than Destiny. The twins were dark-skinned black girls with long straight weaves that reached the end of their backs. Both girls were curvy with big hips and small waists.

I looked the new girls over, feeling unimpressed with their outfits. We all gathered in the makeup room while I went over the house rules and reminded them that they were on a probationary period. I also reminded them that this was my house and at any time I felt disrespected, or they weren't earning their keep, they would be put out. The girls all nodded to show they understood. I gave a quick tour of the house and showed them their assigned bedrooms. I explained my bedroom and the garage were both off limits. Coffee often kept his product in the garage before it was transferred out of town, so the only people who had access to the garage were his staff.

"I'm sure excited to be working with you. Ain't nothing like working the streets and not having no place to go at the end of the night," Trish said looking around excitedly.

"Don't get too comfortable, Chica, you still gotta prove yourself," Erica reminded coldly.

"I ain't never had a problem turning tricks," Trish bragged. "I've been a working girl since I was thirteen."

"Yeah, Chica, but you ain't never worked for Mia before," Erica retorted.

"No I haven't, but this ain't my first rodeo," Trish said standing her ground.

"Leave her alone, Erica! You don't run shit but your mouth, so stop trying to pretend like she need your damn advice," Blondie snapped.

Erica began to respond when I cut her off, "Y'all should start getting ready for work."

I went to my room to try on my new outfits.

I got first in the shower," Brandy announced rushing towards the bathroom.

"I call next," Nikki said biting her thumbnail.

"Just use that smaller bathroom downstairs," Miracle suggested.

"Yeah," Destiny agreed.

"Cause when she get out, we got next," Miracle informed her.

"Alright," Nikki complied.

"Wait, you Chicas shower together?" Erica asked with disgust.

"Yeah, why?" the twins asked in unison. The other girls laughed.

"Let them shower together, more hot water for the rest of us," Trish said laughing at her own joke.

"I didn't ask for nobody's opinion and we don't need permission to take a shower," Miracle said taking offense.

Nikki grabbed her bag and sheepishly headed down the stairs.

"Y'all notice how scared she looked? That Chica won't be catching no Johns," Erica stated shaking her head.

"Why you so worried about what she doing?" Miracle asked.

"Yeah, worry about yourself," Destiny advised.

"Oh, hell no! I'm not gonna be getting checked by the Double Mint Twins!" Erica said rolling her neck and crossing her arms.

Trish began to snicker.

"You're gonna let your mouth get you in trouble," Miracle warned.

Erica rolled her eyes and left the room.

"Well, let's all go downstairs and take some shots!" Blondie suggested.

The girls bickering was a constant over the next few months. I had a lot of different girls come and go in the course of six months. Nikki was kicked out on her third day in the house, when I caught her stealing. Her purse fell off the countertop while I was cooking, and all its contents spilled out on the floor. When I went to put her stuff back inside, I saw my favorite diamond stud earrings which I thought I'd misplaced. I picked them up and put them in my pocket.

When Nikki came downstairs looking like her usual timid self I asked, "Nikki have you seen my diamond earrings?"

"Me?" she asked innocently.

"I figured you might have seen 'em since they were in your purse," I said calmly.

Nikki started to run, but I caught her by her arm and spun her around to face me.

"Get your shit, and get the hell out of my house! And if you take anything that belongs to me on your way out, I will hunt you down and cut off every finger on your sneaky little hands," I threatened.

Nikki pulled away from my grip, grabbed her purse, and ran out of the front door. Inside her backpack that she'd left upstairs, I found a pair of my sandals, my hairbrush and my cell phone charger. I put her things back inside and threw the whole bag in the trash and called Coffee.

"If you want me to take care of it, just let me know. You have to make an example out of her, Mia, so the other girls don't just think they can get over on you," Coffee lectured.

"No, I don't want her hurt. I just needed her gone. Can you tell your guys to do a better check on these girls before we move anymore bottom of the barrel bitches into my house?" I asked angrily.

"It's not like these girls come with a college degree and a page of references, Mia. The seven-day trial is only to make sure they can work and get money," Coffee explained.

"More like take money," I mumbled.

"In the meantime, I need you to stop playing nice, Mia, and make sure the girls know who they're working for," Coffee instructed.

After that day, I became a lot less trusting. All the girls were subject to random searches conducted by Rick and Maurice, whenever I felt like someone was being sneaky. I also stopped allowing the girls to call me by my name and instead they were to address me as "Madam." I didn't engage in small talk, or sit in on their petty arguments. I kept our relationship strictly professional. Whenever I entered the room all the working girls would get quiet. I started monitoring the track alongside Rick and Maurice so I could see who was grinding and who was just making enough to meet their quota.

One night while monitoring, I noticed Destiny wasn't much use to me. She was kind of a dead weight on Miracle's hustle. All their clients were getting two for the price of one.

Not on my dime they wouldn't! This was just bad business and unacceptable. I warned Destiny to be more assertive and to step it up, or she would have to get out. Miracle said that if her sister goes she goes. I shrugged with indifference. I was glad to see she had some sense of loyalty, but even gladder to see she was a smart girl. She went back on her threat to leave when her sister was kicked out the next week. Destiny had not been able to meet her quota without Miracles help.

I'd gotten so involved in the business and used to my responsibilities as a Madam, that when I checked the mail and saw the invitation to attend Mama's wedding, I thought about not going. I was focused on our hustle, and I didn't want to be reminded of the past. However, after I thought about how supportive Coffee was at his mother's wedding, I considered going. But, I wasn't looking forward to it.

Mama was happy. She'd gotten Daddy to sign the divorce papers and she could move on with her life. She no longer had to work two jobs and was able to go back to school to become a registered nurse. She'd always dreamt of working in the hospital as a nurse, but when she met Daddy, she gave up her dreams. She became the housewife that Daddy wanted.

Now that she was with James, she was able to take night courses to get her degree.

James owned a barbershop on Central Avenue, and he made a decent income. I just didn't understand why he drove such a raggedy car, but he could support Mama and Junior with his income from the shop. When Mama told me he'd paid for her to go back to school, I realized it wasn't James I hated as much as it was the idea of James. He was a constant reminder to me that my daddy wasn't around, and he was just so corny and easy to hate. Deep down, I was happy that Mama had someone in her life that made her happy, and Junior would have a father figure in his life growing up.

It had been a year since we moved to Sundown Valley and I was fully adjusted to my new lifestyle and reputation. I walked in the house, shuffling through the mail, which was mostly sales papers. When I reached the top of the stairs, I saw that my bedroom door was wide open. I was surprised, but figured Coffee must have snuck inside while I was checking the mail.

"Babe?" I called entering the room and not seeing Coffee in sight.

I noticed the bathroom door was slightly open. I pushed it all the way open and saw Brandy on the bathroom floor hugging the toilet.

"What the hell are you doing in my bathroom?" I asked annoyed.

"The other bathrooms were occupied, and I was feeling sick," she explained.

"That's not my problem!" I snapped.

"If you guys didn't spend your days getting wasted..."

"I'm not wasted," Brandy denied.

"Then why the hell are you puking your guts out in my toilet?" I asked becoming impatient.

"I'm pregnant!" Brandy yelled before gripping the toilet and throwing up the contents in her stomach.

I looked away, feeling my own urge of nausea from hearing Brandy vomit.

"You gotta get the hell outta here!" I said unsympathetically.

"What?" Brandy asked wiping her mouth.

"You heard me. You gotta get your shit and get the hell out."

"You would throw me out when I'm the best girl you got in this whole house?" Brandy asked in disbelief.

"Everyone is replaceable, Brandy, even you. And what the hell did you think would happen? You're no good to me with morning sickness and when you start showing, do you really think you can work the track with a damn baby bump? The fact that you told me about your pregnancy lets me know that you have every intention on keeping it, so there's really nothing for us to discuss."

"You think you can just throw me out? Well, it won't be that easy," Brandy said flushing the toilet and standing up.

"Bitch, please. I'll throw you and all your shit out of my house."

"And you'll be sorry!" Brandy said knowingly.

"Are you threatening me?" I asked getting ready for a fight.

"No, I'm not threatening you, but I'm not going nowhere, Madam Mia. I'm here to stay," Brandy said smugly.

"This is Coffee's baby."

"What?!" I asked in disbelief.

"You gotta be kidding me! You're a hooker Brandy. You lay down with anything with a dollar. Why the hell would I believe you?"

At that moment Coffee appeared in the doorway.

"What's going on in here?" he asked looking from me to Brandy.

"I'm so glad you're home, Babe. This tramp is claiming that

she's pregnant with your baby!" I exclaimed looking at Brandy with disgust.

"Go ahead, Coffee, tell her." Brandy said crossing her arms.

"You have some nerve!" I yelled as I lunged at Brandy grabbing a fist full of her hair.

I was pulled back by Coffee,

"Stop Mia! She's pregnant!"

"With your child?" I asked turning to face him. Coffee looked uncomfortable, and guilty.

"Coffee, tell me this hooker is not carrying your child!" I demanded through clenched teeth.

Brandy stood there with a smirk on her face enjoying every minute of the scene that was about to erupt into chaos.

"Mia, you just need to calm down," Coffee said.

I started swinging and clawing at Coffee's face. I clawed him and hit him in the face with my closed fist. He blocked my hits and attempted to catch my wrist.

"Mia! Mia! Stop!" he yelled as he restrained me by my wrist.

I kneed him in his groin, forcing him to stumble forward losing his hold on my wrist. I began to punch Coffee on his head and back as he struggled to recover from the blow to his genitals. Rick and Maurice heard the commotion and ran upstairs in time to see me knee Coffee in his face as he was still bent forward.

Maurice swooped in and grabbed me by my waist as I kicked and clawed to get free from his hold. Coffee stood up with a bloody nose and busted lip.

"Mia, what the hell is wrong with you?!" he demanded.

"Let me go!" I yelled as I continued to struggle against his hold. Coffee wiped his nose, seeing his own blood smeared on his fingers.

"Let her go," Coffee ordered.

I continued to kick and resist to no avail.

"I said let her go!"

He let me go, and I stood across from Coffee, panting and trying to catch my breath.

Brandy's eyes were wide with fear, but I knew she was telling the truth by the look on Coffee's face.

"Get the hell out of my house!" I yelled at Coffee vehemently.

"You and your hooker better get your shit, and get out!"

"Mia, wait..."

"Shut up! After I stuck by you through everything, you would do this to me?! All those talks about loyalty and respect! Well, you have no loyalty and you clearly have no respect for me! So, take your tramp, and get the hell out of my house!" I screamed.

Brandy had become scared for her own safety and was hiding behind Coffee for protection.

Coffee didn't argue. He just moved toward the door and Brandy followed close behind like a scared puppy dog.

"Get out!" I yelled at Rick and Maurice, who were looking confused at what they had just witnessed. "And don't you ever put your hands on me again!" I yelled before slamming the bedroom door and locking it.

I sank down in front of the door feeling angry and betrayed. I was shaking, and my heart was still racing. I began to cry and I felt as though I would never be able to stop.

Ten

I hadn't left my bedroom in days. I stayed curled up in my bed with my door locked and my curtains drawn. My cell phone battery died, so I had no contact with the outside world which is exactly what I wanted. A few times I heard knocks on my bedroom door which I ignored until whoever it was got the hint and left. I'd only gotten up to use the bathroom and then I'd crawl back in bed, pulling my covers over my head not wanting to be awake. Rick and Maurice continued to slip envelopes of the girl's profits underneath my door. There were multiple envelopes that were starting to pile up, but I didn't bother to pick them up or count my money.

One evening, I heard someone at my door.

"Go away," I mumbled.

To my surprise I heard the door open and then close. I pulled the covers from my head and saw Trish standing in sweatpants and a t-shirt holding a tray of food.

"I hope you don't mind that I picked your lock. I was just so worried about you, Madam," she explained in her southern accent.

She walked towards me carrying a tray of chicken noodle soup, saltine crackers, and a glass of orange juice.

"I figured if you weren't up here dead, you'd be dying of hunger," Trish said laughing at her own joke.

I sat up with no energy to argue or protest.

"Oh! Madam, you look terrible!" Trish exclaimed and then retracted, "I'm sorry. I didn't mean it like that. It's just you're usually so put together," Trish rambled on.

"Here have something to eat. I made you some soup and crackers because my Nana used to say this here is food for the soul, and it can cure any sickness or cold."

Trish climbed on my bed beside me.

I looked at the food in front of me and realized I hadn't eaten in days, but I hadn't had an appetite. I ignored the spoon on the tray and picked up the bowl and drank the soup. I could feel the warm broth travel down my throat and fill my empty stomach. With every gulp, I gained a little bit more energy. I drank the whole glass of orange juice as Trish watched with wide eyes.

When I was done, I passed her the tray and said, "Trish, I know that you know I'm not sick."

"Well sometimes heartache can be just as painful as a stomachache," Trish said knowingly, confirming my suspicions that all the other girls knew and were talking about my business.

"Thanks, Trish, but can you close my door on your way out?" I said before lying back down and rolling over and pulling up my covers.

"Sure," Trish said climbing off my bed and heading toward the door.

"I really don't mean to be in your business but..."

"Then don't!" I said coldly.

Trish got the hint and left, closing the door behind her.

The food made me feel more alive, and I decided I would leave my darkest days behind me and move forward. My heart was still hurting from the betrayal, but I knew it would heal. I dragged myself out of bed and took a hot shower after putting my cell phone on the charger.

The warm water was exactly what I needed to clear my head. I didn't cry another tear, they were all dried up.

As I sat in front of my mirror at my vanity table staring back at my reflection, I wondered what my next move would be. I struggled with the idea of tossing all the girls out of my house, but that would be pure spite. Once I separated my emotions from the situation, I realized the money I was making as a Madam was funding my lavish lifestyle that I'd become very accustomed to.

I covered my puffy eyes with foundation powder, applied eyeliner and lipstick. I was beginning to look more like myself I thought, as I brushed the tangles out of my hair and pulled it into a high bun. I dressed in a short yellow sundress and sandals. I grabbed my cell phone and purse and headed downstairs. I was happy to see all the girls were outside lounging by the pool. I grabbed my car keys and left, noticing Rick was in his car parked in front of the house.

Coffee had left seventeen voicemail messages on my phone over the last few days. I deleted them all, unwilling to hear his voice or what he had to say. To sleep with one of the working girls was bad enough, but to not even use protection? That was just unacceptable. I wasn't convinced Brandy's unborn child was his, but the fact that it was even a possibility made me cringe. I knew I would eventually have to talk to

Coffee, because we were running a business together. It would be hard to separate our romantic relationship from our business relationship, but it had to be done.

When I arrived at Mama's apartment, I saw Junior outside on the steps playing with his trucks.

"Junior," I called, pulling him from playing.

"Hey, Mia!" Junior shouted, running down the steps to my car window.

"Get in," I said unlocking the door.

"Wow, Mia, you have a cool car!"

"Why are you outside by yourself?"

"Cause Jacob and Tati had to go home."

"Where's Mama?"

"In class."

"Where's James?"

"He in the house asleep. He said he had a long day," Junior informed me.

"So, do you like James?" I asked

"Yeah, James let me help out at the barbershop."

"Junior you know how to cut hair?" I teased.

"Yeah, but he just let me sweep and change the channels on the T.V." Junior said proudly.

"Oh does he pay you good?" I asked enjoying Junior's company.

"Nope, but sometimes he get me candy."

"Is that why all your teeth are falling out?" I asked jokingly.

"Mama said when you lose your teeth it just means you getting older."

"Oh. okay," I said with a nod.

"So, how's Tati?"

"She's good."

"Is Tati your girlfriend?" I asked.

Junior made a face,

"That's gross Mia! She's not my girlfriend. But Jacob said he has a girlfriend."

"Oh really? What about you? Do you have a girlfriend?"

"No Mia, I don't want no girlfriend!"

"Alright, alright, I had to ask," I said trying not to laugh.

"I just wanted to check on you, and make sure you're alright," I said rubbing Junior's curly hair.

"Yeah I'm alright," Junior said.

"What about you? Are you alright, Mia?"

"Yeah, I'm alright," I said forcing a smile.

"Go on and go play, I'll see you next weekend at Mama's wedding."

"Okay, bye, Mia," Junior said opening the car door and hopping out.

"Take your toys inside and play, it's getting dark," I instructed through the open window.

"Alright," Junior collected his trucks from the steps.

When I pulled up to Grandma Trudy's house, it looked as though the whole house was dark except for the flickering light from the television. I figured Grandma Trudy was probably watching one of her shows, so I decided to park and go inside. I knocked and Tati opened the door.

"Mia!" she exclaimed, hugging my legs.

"Hey, Tati," I said, coming inside and shutting the door.

"Where's Grandma?"

"Gram ain't feeling good. She's in bed," Tati explained as she grabbed my fingers and led me towards the T.V.

"What you watching?"

"Dell the Dinosaur just went off but there's another show about to come on next!" Tati said excitedly.

"I'm gonna go check on Grandma, I'll be right back," I said walking down the hallway to Grandma Trudy's room. Her door was slightly ajar so I knocked softly letting myself in.

"Grandma, you sleep? It's Mia," I said as I entered the dark room.

"Hey, Baby, I didn't hear you come in," she said from her bed in a low husky voice.

"Tati let me in. How are you feeling?" I asked as I sat at the foot of her bed.

"Oh, I'm hanging in there," Grandma Trudy said in a hoarse whisper.

"Grandma, you don't look so good. Have you been to the doctor?" I asked with concern.

"Yeah, I went, but those pills they gave don't seem to work. They say I got pneumonia in my lungs," Grandma coughed forcefully.

"Let me get you some water."

"No, Baby, I'm fine. You just sit on down and tell me how you been?" Grandma said before she was interrupted by another coughing spell.

"I'm worried about you."

"I'll be alright," Grandma Trudy said with a strained voice.

"Grandma, I'm going to send a nurse over here in the morning to look after you, until you're feeling better. She can cook your meals and help you take your medicine."

"Oh, Baby, I don't have no insurance to cover nothing like that," Grandma Trudy protested.

"Don't worry about that, Grandma, just focus on getting better. Is it alright if I take Tati with me? She can stay with me while you get better, and I'll bring her back with me next weekend when I come for Mama's wedding if that's alright?"

"Oh, Baby, you don't have to do that," Grandma Trudy objected.

"I want to."

"Well, if she gets to be too much, you just bring her right on back." Grandma Trudy instructed.

"Alright," I agreed.

I warmed up soup and placed a water pitcher and cup at her bedside. Tati helped me pack her bag and she added some of her favorite toys. Tati was thrilled to get to spend a week with me. She talked nonstop all the way back to Sundown Valley.

When I pulled into my driveway, Tati was snoring. I saw Maurice was now the one parked in front of the house in his car, and I waved him over to help me. He carried Tati in and I carried her bag, following close behind. If she woke up, I didn't want her to be frightened.

"Lay her down in my bed," I instructed, once we were inside.

The house was quiet and it felt peaceful because all the girls were out on the track. I took Tati's shoes off and covered her with my blanket. I left the light on and went downstairs.

Maurice was on his way back outside to his car when I asked, "Where's Rick?"

"He's watching the track," Maurice informed me.

"Where's Coffee?" I asked with a straight face.

"He'll be back in town tomorrow," Maurice confessed.

"Are all the girls gone?" I asked.

"Yeah they all left about two hours ago." Maurice answered raising his eyebrows at my line of questioning.

"Well then, we're alone?"

"Yeah, what's up?" Maurice asked looking confused.

"Have a drink with me," I said.

Maurice smiled.

"Naw, you know I can't," he protested.

"Come on!" I pleaded. "It'll be our little secret."

Maurice reluctantly followed me to the bar and I kicked off my sandals.

"Loosen up Maurice! I won't bite." I said flirtatiously.

Maurice smiled as I poured us both a shot.

"To new beginnings," I said clinking glasses with Maurice before swallowing the shot in one gulp. Maurice did the same.

"Let's take another!" I smiled.

After two more shots I was feeling good. We laughed and talked feeling tipsy.

"Guess what, Maurice?" I said not waiting for him to answer, "I have a secret stash in the kitchen," I admitted giggling.

"Secret stash of what? Cash?"

"No silly!" I said going to the kitchen and bringing back a zip-lock bag of weed.

"Oh well, aren't you the rebel," Maurice said sarcastically.

I pulled a bong from underneath the cabinet and we

smoked and laughed at each other doing impersonations of the staff and the girls.

I laughed until my sides ached. Maurice became attractive to me as I sat against the wall behind the bar, passing the bong and reminiscing. Maurice was caught off guard as I leaned in and kissed him passionately, before he even had time to exhale his smoke.

Maurice began to cough and scrambled to get to his feet. I stood up, pushing him against the wall. I started kissing him again, first on the lips and then on his neck as I stood on my tiptoes.

Before I knew it I was pulling my sundress over my head and he was struggling to undo his belt buckle. In the heat of our passion we managed to break the bong, several bottles of alcohol, and a few shot glasses.

Maurice held me up against the wall as I locked my legs around his waist and allowed him to enter me. We had the most passionate sex I'd ever experienced. The mixture of weed and alcohol in my system heightened all of my senses and I felt pleasures that I'd never known.

Maurice exploded inside of me and we both slid down the wall panting. We were surrounded by broken glass and puddles of alcohol that were the result of our sexscapade.

I got up first, picking up my panties and dress from the floor. Maurice sat with a look of disbelief on his face.

"Mia, I..." Maurice began.

"Shhh," I silenced him, not caring to hear what he had to say.

"I just...I really need this job," Maurice explained.

"Don't worry," I said before heading upstairs to the shower.

"It will be our little secret."

Eleven

I felt no regrets the next morning other than a slight headache from all the alcohol. I was feeling renewed. Even though I didn't plan on sharing the events of last night with Coffee, I was glad they had taken place. Revenge sex felt so much better than makeup sex I concluded.

"Mia, what's for breakfast?" Tati asked as soon as she'd woken up.

"You gotta get up, take a bath and brush your teeth, Tati, and then we'll eat breakfast."

"Alright." Tati whined.

I ran Tati's bubble bath while I placed a call to a home health agency in Grandma Trudy's area.

"This is Comfort Care Home Health Agency. How may I direct your call?" the receptionist asked politely.

"My grandma is sick and I would like to hire nursing staff to care for her around the clock. She doesn't have health insurance, so I'll be paying for her care out of pocket. I would like all the bills sent to my address," I explained before the receptionist placed me on hold to collect more information.

After we'd both gotten ready, I took Tati downstairs and made her pancakes.

"You're pretty," Tati said looking at Blondie.

"Thanks girl," Blondie said popping her bubble gum and peeling an orange.

"You have big boobs," Tati added giggling.

"Yeah, they cost big bucks!"

I glared at Blondie and she went back to peeling her orange.

"I can't wait 'til I got boobs," Tati said eating her pancakes with her fingers.

"Why do you want boobs?" I asked raising my eyebrows.

"So I can be pretty too."

"I think you're pretty now."

"Thanks, Mia," Tati said smiling.

"Tati, we're gonna go shopping when you're done eating. We have to get an outfit for my mama's wedding."

"Okay, I won't beg for nothing," Tati said as if that notion had been drilled into her memory.

"What?" I asked caught off guard by her comment. "Tati, when you're with me, you can ask for whatever you want."

"Really?" Tati asked in disbelief.

"Yeah, really."

"Are you gonna drive your Barbie car?" Tati asked.

"Yeah, but it's not a Barbie car, Tati. It's a Bentley."

"Oh, well it's pretty," Tati said licking syrup from her chubby fingers.

As I was backing out of the driveway, Coffee pulled up behind me, blocking me in. I rolled down the windows and turned on my stereo.

"I'll be right back, Tati," I said before getting out of the car, crossing my arms.

"Mia, we need to talk."

"Coffee, I don't have time for this. I have Tati in the backseat and I don't want to fight in front of her."

"Mia, I'm not trying to fight. I only wanna talk. Where you headed?"

"We're going to the mall," I answered rolling my eyes.

"Can I join you?"

"Shouldn't you be tending to your baby mama?"

"Come on, Mia, you know we need to talk."

"Is it about the business? Because that's the only conversation I'm having with you," I informed him.

"Okay, so when can we talk business?" he asked smoothly.

"I'll be home tonight. Now, can you please move your car? I have to go."

"Alright, I'll see you tonight. I love you," Coffee said before getting into his car.

That night, Coffee came over for a few hours after the girls had all left for their shift, and Tati had fallen asleep upstairs watching Disney movies. I sat at the kitchen table smoking a cigarette when Coffee used his key to let himself in.

"Hey, Mia," Coffee said with a smile.

"I really need to change those locks," I said underneath my breath.

"Alright, Mia, enough is enough. I gave you your space, and I've been patient with you because I know I hurt you. But, we gotta move on."

"Move on? There is no moving on, Coffee! What you did is unforgivable," I said shaking my head in disgust.

"Mia, I'm sorry. I'm not a perfect man. I messed up. I know

you haven't stopped loving me. Just give me a chance to make this right," Coffee pleaded.

"I thought we were gonna talk business," I said, ignoring his apology.

"Okay, Mia, if you're gonna continue to be distant, how can I trust you to handle your end of the business?"

"Trust me?! I'm not the one who was dishonest and disloyal," I snapped.

"How many times are you gonna throw that in my face?" Coffee asked losing his patience.

"You made me look like a fool!" I yelled.

"You told me to command respect from these girls, and the whole time you were sleeping with her behind my back! How many other working girls have you slept with?"

Coffee didn't respond.

"All of them?" I asked accusingly standing up and putting my hands on my hips.

"Mia, there's just no getting through to you," Coffee said shaking his head.

"Unless we're talking business, we have nothing to talk about," I said rolling my eyes.

Coffee sighed and then said, "Alright, Mia, we'll do this your way. You continue to handle your end of the business, and I'll handle mine. My staff and I will still need access to the garage, but if it makes you feel better, you can change the locks on the front door."

"I don't need your staff in front of my house, watching my every move."

"As much as I like knowing that you're safe, my security

ain't just for you, Mia. I have a lot of money coming in and out of here, so I have to protect my investments."

"Alright, but your staff can use the back exit to access the garage, and what I do on my personal time is none of your concern."

"Alright. We can respect each other's privacy. I'm just glad I still get to see you. Business or not, the pleasure is all mine," Coffee said as he stepped closer to me, invading my personal space.

"Coffee, you should go," I said feeling my heart yearn for his touch.

He lifted my chin and leaned down to kiss my lips, but I pulled away standing my ground.

"Let yourself out," I said turning away and going upstairs to check on Tati.

It felt good to get back to living my life on my terms. I enjoyed my relationship with Coffee, but I had a sense of relief that I no longer had the "girlfriend" title and I was free to live life as a single woman. I felt empowered and ready to move on. I no longer lived under Coffee's reputation, but I had earned my own.

I was known as "Madam Mi" on the streets. When I was out, I'd receive admiring looks from every guy in my path and envious stares from every female. Sundown Valley was a small town, and word travelled fast. It didn't take long for the streets to be buzzing that Madam Mi was no longer taken by the infamous drug lord, Coffee. With the split of the "most talked about power couple," I became the most eligible bachelorette in town. But, I was not searching for love; I was just looking to have fun.

"Hey, Madam Mi. It's good to see you. Shelly is all ready for your three o'clock. She'll be right with you," the receptionist at Styles by Shelly greeted me, as I entered the beauty salon.

"Hi, Denise, did you remember that I also have an appointment for my goddaughter, Tati?" I asked removing my shades.

"Oh, you're right," Denise acknowledged flipping through her appointment log.

"You ladies go on and make yourself comfortable. She'll be right up," Denise said with a smile.

I took Tati's hand and led her to the waiting area, where she followed my lead in picking a magazine from the rack.

"Right this way, Madam Mi. Did you ladies want something to drink?" Shelly asked, waving us to the back towards her chair.

"I'll have bottled water," I said glancing down at Tati to see what she wanted.

"I'm fine," Tati said shyly.

"Well, aren't you cute!" Shelly squealed looking at Tati.

"We have a new wash girl, so let me know if she's up to your standard," Shelly whispered as she passed me a cold water bottle from the mini fridge.

"If you trust her to work in your shop, I'm sure she's fine," I said with a smile.

Tati got settled in her seat as Shelly began to take out her braids and burettes.

"Are you ready to be washed?" A tall, light-skinned woman asked. We both did a double-take as we recognized each other.

"Justine?" I asked surprised.

"Hey girl," Justine said forcing a smile.

"You know my new wash girl?" Shelly asked eavesdropping.

"Oh yeah, we go way back I said," flashing a smile at Justine.

I hadn't seen her since our schoolyard fight when I was in the 7th grade, but she looked the same with her light skin, green eyes, and freckled face.

I was happy to see she finally tamed her wild hair. It was still light brown but she wore it pressed straight, and it hung halfway down her back. I noticed she had a light scar on her forehead and I couldn't help but wonder if it was the result of her bullying me.

"Wow, small world," Shelly went on, "Jessy, didn't you say you just moved here from out of town?" Shelly asked being nosy.

"Yeah, I'm still new to the Valley," Justine admitted.

"Well, ain't that something. You happen to know Madam Mi, one of the most well-known girls in town," Shelly exclaimed with a smile.

Justine forced a smile, feeling uncomfortable.

"I'm ready for my wash," I said changing the subject.

"Right this way," Justine said leading me to the wash chair.

"As far as I'm concerned, we're old friends," I said with a wink as soon as Shelly was out of earshot.

Justine covered me with a pink smock and asked, "How do you like your water temperature?" looking relieved.

After my wash, Justine led me to the dryers and I tipped her a Benjamin. Tati was so excited to be at the salon and she'd warmed up to the unfamiliar faces. I could see her talking Shelly's ear off, and although I couldn't hear what she was saying, I could tell she was keeping Shelly entertained.

It was my turn in Shelly's chair, and she was happy when I turned down my usual press and flat-iron and instead opted for a 28-inch Brazilian hair weave with highlights. My new hair style was a testament to my new found freedom.

"Dag, girl, you look really good," Justine complimented me on my new look as I checked it out in the mirror.

"Thanks, girl, I needed a new look for my new beginning," I said with a smile.

Justine looked puzzled.

"Bad breakup," I explained, sure she'd hear about it eventually in this small town of loud mouths.

"Oh...well I'm sure he'll be kicking himself when he sees you," Justine said admiring my look.

"Yeah, well I'm gonna let him eat his heart out," I laughed.

"So, how's your family?" I asked, indirectly asking about her cousin, Candy.

"Fine I guess," Justine said with a shrug.

"I just had to get away, start a new beginning of my own," Justine explained.

"Well you should come out with me this weekend."

"Where you going?"

"Whatever club or lounge holds my attention," I said with a smile.

"My friend use to say, 'If it ain't packed, it's probably whack!'" I said quoting Sasha.

We both laughed and traded numbers agreeing to go out that weekend.

Tati climbed down from Shelly's chair with a big smile on

her face. She kept running her fingers through her hair and flipping it over her shoulders.

"I've never worn my hair straight before." Tati said, staring at her reflection in the mirror.

I tipped Shelly and paid for our hairstyles at the receptionist desk.

"Put us down for a touch up early Saturday morning. We have an out of town wedding to go to."

"Okay, how about 9 a.m.?" Denise asked.

"That's fine. Thanks, Denise," I said taking Tati's hand and walking out of the salon as Tati skipped beside me.

Twelve

On the day of Mama's wedding, I was running late. Tati and I had got caught in traffic on our way to the courthouse, so I wasn't able to see Mama beforehand. I slipped into the courthouse with Tati and took a seat up front next to Junior. He smiled at me and stuck his tongue out at Tati, who playfully returned the gesture.

Mama looked nice wearing an ivory lace wedding gown with pearl earrings and necklace. She'd opted for a pair of ivory flats, probably because James was so short. He was beaming as he held Mama's hand promising to love, honor, and cherish her.

It was bittersweet to witness their love. I couldn't help but wonder if Daddy would have understood why I decided to come. I didn't want to betray Daddy, but since I also didn't wanna hurt Mama, I was going to be left feeling guilty no matter what. After the ceremony, we went to Mama's apartment for the reception. James hired a D.J. and the guests helped themselves to barbeque chicken, corn on the cob and potato salad. The apartment was packed with family and friends. All of the furniture had been moved out of the house and was replaced with rented folding chairs that lined the walls for the guests to sit.

However, most of the guests crowded into the kitchen talking and laughing while they held their plates, or they were doing the electric slide in the middle of the living room floor.

My Auntie Glen came from out of town and brought all six of her rowdy kids. They were running in and out of the apartment, chasing each other with the light blue balloons that were once decoration but were now being used like napkins by their chubby, barbeque sauce stained fingers.

I was happy to see that Mama's wedding present was being delivered right on time. I went into the kitchen and had to practically drag Mama out of the house and down the steps away from her clingy guests.

"Congratulations, Mama!" I said handing her keys to a new model of the Honda that had been dragged away nearly eight years ago.

"Oh my goodness!" Mama said with a puzzled expression.

"Mama, this is your wedding present," I explained.

"Girl, I can't accept this," Mama shook her head in protest. "I don't know how you got it, but take it back."

"Mama, it's paid for."

"With what? Your boyfriend's drug money?" Mama accused.

"It's a nice gesture, Mia, it really is, but I can't accept it," Mama refused.

"Mama, the car is yours! Can't nobody take this one. It's in your name. Let me do this for you, Mama. You don't owe nobody nothing. It's a gift," I explained putting the car keys in Mama's hand and closing her fingers around them.

"Lord child, you never cease to amaze me. I don't even know how to thank you," Mama said with tears in her eyes while wrapping her arms around me and squeezing me tight.

Once word had spread inside the house of Mama's wedding present, everyone migrated outside to ooh and aah over the car.

I heard Auntie Glen ask, "How'd she get that kind of money?"

"That ain't nothing! Did you see the car she was driving?" one of Mama's nosey friends answered.

Someone came outside and broke up all the gossip and spectators by announcing, "They're getting ready to cut the cake!"

By the time I got back upstairs, Mama and James both had frosting on their faces and they were giggling like kids. I heard my mama laugh more that night than I had in my whole life. She was happy.

I was surprised to see Grandma Trudy come out of the kitchen holding a plate.

"Hey, Grandma! I didn't even see you come in, how you feeling?"

"I'm hanging in there," Grandma Trudy said with a smile.

She looked good. She wore a long lavender dress and had her grey hair swept up into a French corn roll.

"I'm glad you're feeling better."

"Yeah, you can't keep an old dog down for too long," Grandma Trudy said with a laugh. "Thank you for taking care of Tati, and for sending over them nurses. I am so grateful."

"No problem, Grandma. I'm gonna miss Tati. I really enjoyed spending so much time with her."

"Yeah, she's something else." Grandma Trudy said with a smile.

Just then Tati ran towards us holding a big piece of cake. Tati had played so hard that nearly all her curls had fallen out, and she had barbeque sauce on her dress and frosting on her fingers.

"Gram, Tony said I got a big head," Tati told.

"Come on, Tati, let's get you cleaned up," I said taking the cake plate.

"Thank you, Mia," Grandma Trudy said shaking her head.

I took Tati inside the bathroom and washed her hands and face. I used a hair tie from my purse and pulled her hair into a ponytail.

"Thanks, Mami," Tati said attempting to say "Madam Mi."

"No problem, Tati. Thank you for visiting me. I want you to take good care of your Gram."

"You're about to go, Mami?" Tati asked disappointed.

"Yeah, I gotta drive back to the Valley before it gets too late."

"Ahhh, man!" Tati whined.

"Remember, Tati, when boys tease you it just means they secretly like you."

She giggled and nodded in agreement. I got her bag out of the car and went back inside to say my goodbyes.

Junior gave me a hug, getting frosting on my dress.

"Bye Mia," he said before returning to his game of tag.

I called Justine on my way back home. She said she was getting ready, so I rushed home to shower and get dressed. I decided on a pair of black short shorts and a midriff-bearing leopard print tank top. I paired my outfit with black stilettos, gold bangles and big gold hoop earrings. I let down my long-highlighted tresses and did my makeup. When Justine arrived, I was already headed downstairs with my purse and car keys.

"Hey Madam Mi, you're looking good," Justine said looking my outfit over.

"Thanks, girl. Your dress is cute," I returned the compliment.

Justine wore a short green dress that accented her curves and she paired it with a low heel. We arrived at the Tilt Lounge and bypassed the line, walking straight to the front.

"Wow, Madam Mi, it looks like you came to party," The bouncer said looking me over.

"Thanks, Darious," I said with a smile.

"This my girl Jess."

He moved the rope allowing us both entry inside. At the bar, we got free drinks, courtesy of management.

"Dang, Madam Mi, you got pull," Justine said as we sipped our drinks.

"I'm not stunting these drinks." Let's see how long it takes for one of these guys to work up the courage to ask us to dance," I said with a laugh.

"Hello, my name is Rodney. You're Madam Mi, right?" A tall, light-skinned guy asked while looking me over.

"Mmhmm", I answered uninterested and scanning the room.

"Can I get you a drink?" he offered.

"I'm drinking one," I said with a smile.

"Right, well your next one is on me," he smiled back.

At that moment, the DJ switched it up and an upbeat song came on.

"Jess, this is my song! Come on, girl, you gotta come dance with me," I said excitedly as Justine reluctantly followed me out to the middle of the dance floor.

I began to move my hips and pop my ass to the beat. Rodney moved in behind me as I danced seductively up against him. Justine began to loosen up as she was approached by a dancing partner of her own. We were the life of the party, and we practically had guys lining up for an opportunity to dance with us. We were having a blast, and would switch dance partners halfway through the song enjoying the attention we were getting. When the music slowed down, I grabbed Justine's hand and pulled her out of the crowd and towards the restroom.

"Girl, I think I drank too much, I gotta pee," I admitted feeling tipsy.

"I've been holding my pee for the last ten minutes!" Justine confessed.

"Why? You must be feeling that guy?" I said with a smirk.

"Which one?" Justine laughed.

"The one that's been in your face all night," I said as we reached the restroom.

We entered and saw that all three stalls were occupied.

"Justine, I can't hold it," I said pacing.

"Pee in the sink!"

"I'm not peeing in the sink!"

"Fine, move then cause I gotta go, and I'm gonna pee in the sink!" she said laughing.

I watched as Justine straddled the sink and peed down the drain. I was laughing so hard I almost wet myself. Before Justine could get down, someone came out of the stall and gave her a look of disgust before walking out.

"Who you looking at? You're not even gonna wash your hands? You're nasty!" Justine yelled at the bathroom door.

We both busted up laughing and I ran into the empty stall. On our way out of the restroom, I used my hand sanitizer from my purse and shared some with Justine. We slipped out the back exit, feeling the cold breeze on our exposed arms and legs.

"Why we come out the back?" Justine asked shivering.

"I don't want your stalker to see us leave."

"Yeah right, I think he was more into you."

"When guys are too clingy, it's such a turn off," I said shaking my head.

"I never had so many guys beg me for a dance."

"Let's go to Club Sundown and see if we can break your record," I suggested.

By the time we pulled up, it was almost 2 a.m. and people were starting to pour out into the parking lot discussing where the after party was gonna be. I got out and waved at Xavier. He was a member of Coffee's staff, but I didn't see him often.

"Hey, Madam Mi, you're looking good tonight," he said

looking at my hips and thighs before allowing his eyes to travel slowly up my body and then back down again.

"Thanks, Xavier," I said ignoring his lusting eyes.

"Who you got with you?" he asked peering into my car.

"That's my girl, Jess," I said as Justine waved shyly.

"Damn, Madam Mi! Coffee my boy and all, but you gonna make me break guy code," he laughed.

"Xavier, you're crazy," I said with a smile. "We just came to see if the club was worth our time."

"Well, I'm working security up here tonight, so I didn't have any fun, but it was live."

"Oh, looks like we missed it, so we're gonna grab something to eat and head home."

"Alright, be safe, and if you need anything call me," he said with a wink.

"I will," I said flirtatiously.

We stopped for burgers and fries and then headed to my house.

"Madam Mi, I had so much fun! Call me next time you're going out," Justine said as she walked barefoot to her car holding her heels.

"Bye, Jess!" I yelled, noticing Maurice's car parked a few houses down.

I called his phone.

"Hello?" Maurice answered.

"Hey, I just pulled up,"

"Yeah, I saw that,"

"You wanna walk me to my door?" I asked with a smile.

Maurice hesitated and then said, "Sure," before hanging up. I got out of the car and walked to the front door.

"I thought you wanted me to walk you to your door." Maurice said as he walked up.

"I meant walk me upstairs," I clarified with a smile.

"You're trouble," Maurice said shaking his head.

"Well do you want to get into trouble?" I asked seductively. I opened the door and ran upstairs as Maurice followed behind me.

Thirteen

I was lying out by the pool enjoying the warmth of the sun shining on my back when all of a sudden, a tall figure appeared blocking my sun rays. I shielded my eyes, peering up to see Coffee's tall frame standing over me.

"Mia, we need to talk," he said with a serious tone.

"Well, talk," I said laying back down.

"It's business, Mia. Come inside," he ordered.

"And where are your damn clothes?" he asked while watching me stand up from the lounge chair.

"It's a bikini," I said rolling my eyes.

"Yeah, a thong bikini," Coffee said disapprovingly.

"What? You don't like it?" I asked teasingly as I passed Coffee going inside. His eyes followed me, and then he reluctantly followed.

"I'm serious, Mia. Put some damn clothes on. I can't have you prancing around here half naked, and I got my guys working here," Coffee said getting upset.

"I thought you said we had business to discuss," I said crossing my arms.

"I do but..."

"Well, get to it. I know you didn't come all the way over here to tell me how to dress," I said glaring at him.

"Alright! Let's go upstairs, so we can talk."

"Upstairs?" I asked raising my eyebrows.

"We can talk right here," I said becoming impatient.

At that moment, Rick popped his head in the front door and said, "Boss, everything's accounted for. I'm gonna bring the truck around." He glanced lustfully at my body before closing the door.

Coffee's jaw muscles tightened as they often did when he was trying to control his temper. I smirked at him, enjoying Rick's attention, as I stood barefoot in my small, black, thong bikini. Coffee grabbed me by my wrist and practically dragged me up the stairs into my bedroom.

"What's your problem?" I asked as Coffee flung me on the bed.

"Look, Mia, I don't have time to play this game with you right now. We have to get everything out of the garage and I need you to lay low and pull your girls off the track for a few days."

"A few days? What's going on?" I asked beginning to take Coffee more seriously.

"It looks like the police is going to start an investigation on my turf. I have one of my guys working on the inside, so I'm able to stay three steps ahead of them. Somebody is talking, and they sent an anonymous tip that this is where I stash my business. We have to clear out until things blow over."

"And it will all just blow over in a few days?" I asked unconvinced.

"Yeah, they'll be starting their investigation on Thursday.

If nothing is recovered by the end of the weekend, come Monday they're moving on."

"But unless they have a search warrant they can't come in here," I said defensively.

"Come on, Mia, don't be so naïve. This is the DEA we're talking about, not mall cops. They will come prepared with search warrants in hand and K-9's to sniff the place over."

"So where does this leave me, as far as my end of the business?" I asked becoming worried.

"You're not being investigated. As far as they're concerned, this is only about a drug operation. They don't know about the working girls, and there's no need to put them on to it. There's just too much traffic in and out of this house, so you'll have to pull them from the track. Y'all can all go out of town for a few days."

"Out of town!"

"Mia, just think of it as a little vacation," Coffee said convincingly.

"I'll pay for everything. Just tell me how many plane tickets you need and where you want to vacation."

I bit my lip, as I thought everything over.

"How about a resort in Miami?"

"Alright, just call the travel agent and book it. I need everybody gone no later than tomorrow, so my guys will have time to do a walk-through, and so we'll be ready for Thursday."

"Aren't you coming?" I asked, worried about Coffee's well-being.

"No, I need to stay out here to make sure everything goes

smoothly, but I'll send one of my guys with you to make sure y'all straight."

"Okay."

"One more thing," Coffee said before opening the door.

"What's that?"

"Put some damn clothes on," Coffee ordered before leaving the room and heading downstairs.

I pulled some jeans on before going to round up the girls. Everyone was sleeping in and was less than happy about being woken up.

"I need everyone to get up and meet me in the makeup room in the next five minutes," I ordered before going into the next room and making the same announcement. The girl's staggered into the room groaning and complaining underneath their breath. They took their seats at their vanity tables looking only half awake.

"Morning Madam," they said in unison as I waited impatiently for Erica who walked in a few moments later, rubbing her eyes.

"Thanks for joining us," I said glaring at her annoyed.

"Now that we're all here, I have an announcement to make. You all have been doing a really good job and I'm impressed," I lied.

"So, to celebrate your hard work, I'm flying you all out to join me on a weeklong vacation to Miami, Florida!"

The girls faces changed from sleepy to shocked. They screamed and shrieked with excitement.

"Oh my god! Do we need a passport?" Blondie asked with wide eyes.

"No, Einstein. Florida isn't outside the United States," Miracle said rolling her eyes.

"When do we leave?" Trish asked excitedly.

"I'm booking flights for tonight, so go pack!" I said before walking out.

I could hear them still screaming and cheering from excitement all the way downstairs. I grabbed my phone off the kitchen table and went outside by the pool.

"Hey, Jess, what you doing?" I asked sitting beside the pool and dangling my feet in the cold water.

"Nothing, I'm just getting ready for work. What you up to?"

"I'm planning a last-minute vacation to Miami. You wanna come?" I asked

"What? When are you going?" she asked surprised.

"Tonight," I said with a laugh.

"Dang! Talk about last minute!"

"Are you down or what? It'll all be paid for, the plane ticket...the resort...the Mai Tai's," I said persuasively.

"Dang, that does sound good, but I gotta work."

"Well, it's a good thing I'm cool with your boss," I said with a laugh.

"Yeah, Shelly's cool, but I just got this job. I'm not trying to get fired."

"Don't worry about it, Jess. If you wanna go, I'll talk to Shelly. When you get off work today, just pack your bags and you can fly out in the morning,"

"Oh my goodness! What am I gonna wear?" Justine shrieked with excitement.

"It's Miami, just pack bathing suits."

Justine laughed.

"I gotta go book some flights. I'll call you tonight with the details,"

"Okay, talk to you soon," Justine said before hanging up.

While packing my suitcase, I couldn't help but wonder who Coffee would send from his security team to escort us on vacation. Maurice and I still had a little secret fling going on, but I knew better than to bring sand to the beach. At least I knew he could keep his mouth shut.

I had never travelled with so many females. Everything took five times as long as it would if I didn't have the girls slowing down the process. The stretch Hummer limo had been waiting for thirty minutes in front of the house as the girls dragged their stuffed suitcases downstairs.

Rick pulled up in his Cadillac Escalade and started to load the suitcases inside his car. He said he was going to follow us to the airport.

"Where's Maurice?" I asked him as he made several trips hauling the bags to his car.

"What? You're not happy to see me?" Rick said with a smile.

"Yeah, I mean no. I was just wondering, because I'm ready to go, and Coffee said he was sending us with security."

"Yeah, that would be me," he informed me lifting an overweight suitcase over his shoulder.

I wore a light pink velour sweat suit with my white and pink Nikes for our late-night travel. Even in my lounge clothes, I still managed to turn heads.

"Hey, my name is Eric. I just wanted to tell you that I think you are very beautiful," A tall Latino man complimented me.

"Thank you," I said forcing a smile.

"Madam Mi, is he bothering you?" Rick asked coming to sit beside me, scaring the guy away.

"Relax, Rick," I said rolling my eyes.

"I'm so afraid to fly," Trish admitted as we waited to board the plane.

"Damn, Chica! You really picked a hell of a time to mention that," Erica said unsympathetically.

"I ain't never flew since I was a little girl, and the plane shook so badly," Trish said with fear in her eyes.

"It's called turbulence, Chica," Erica said with an attitude.

"It still scared the hell out of me!"

"What happened?" Blondie asked with wide eyes.

"Blondie, what the hell do you think happened? Can't you see she's still here?" Miracle asked annoyed.

"Geez, you don't have to bite my head off," Blondie said defensively.

"If you ain't wanna go, you shoulda said something before Madam Mi bought you a ticket," Miracle said.

"I never said I didn't want to go. I said I was afraid to fly." Trish explained.

"Maybe your fat ass should walk," Miracle mumbled.

Erica laughed.

"Why you gotta be so mean, Miracle? Trish is not fat, she's just thick," Blondie said attempting to defend Trish.

"I'm not worried about Miracle, I'm too busy praying for a safe flight," Trish said.

"Way to jinx the plane, Chica!" Erica yelled angrily.

"How the hell is a prayer a jinx? Erica, you're so full of shit," Blondie said.

"I'll show you..." Erica began before I cut her off,

"Can you all just shut up?" I snapped.

"This is supposed to be a vacation!"

I put on my sunshades and curled up in my seat to attempt a short nap. Before I knew it, I was being shaken awake by Rick.

"Come on, Madam Mi. We're boarding."

"If Coffee ever asks your opinion on a gift, tell him I want a private jet," I said stretching.

"Okay, I'll keep that in mind," Rick said with a chuckle.

Fourteen

When Justine arrived the next day, I was well rested and ready to have fun! We decided to spend most of the day laid out on the beach.

"I can't believe I let you talk me into this," Justine said as she modestly pulled up her beach towel.

"Relax, Jess, they're just boobs."

"Only you, Madam Mi, would pick a topless beach to sunbathe," Justine complained shaking her head.

"I didn't invent nudity; you do know you were born this way right?" I teased.

"Besides, look around, Jess. You don't have the only boobs on the beach."

"Maybe I wouldn't be so uncomfortable if they were a little bigger. You don't have any problems in that area," Justine said with her green eyes full of envy.

"That's why I bought mine," Blondie interjected as she popped her bubblegum.

"Yeah, no thanks," Justine said rolling her eyes.

"Lighten up, Jess! You're so conservative. You have to let your hair down and live a little," I persuaded.

Justine exhaled slowly and took her towel off.

"Okay, I guess I can step out of my comfort zone a little," Justine agreed.

"Madam Mi, you're so spontaneous. Did you really plan all this last minute?"

"Yeah, sometimes you just need to get away," I said with a shrug.

"How did you get Shelly to give me these days off?"

"She owed me a few favors."

Justine raised her eyebrows.

"For what?" she asked curiously.

"Well, a few months ago, I wanted to invest in a business I believed in. When I heard Shelly's salon was going through a rough patch, I decided to become a silent partner."

"So you own a part of Styles by Shelly?" Justine asked in disbelief.

"It's Shelly's shop. I just helped back it financially. When I come in, I'm a customer."

"Wow, your money must run long," Justine said impressed.

"Yeah, I do alright. But this is our vacation. Let's not talk business."

"Didn't you bring your business on vacation with you?" Justine asked glancing towards Blondie and Miracle.

"We could all use some relaxation. Come on, Jess. Let's get some drinks," I said changing the subject.

"Alright," Justine agreed, wrapping her beach towel around her.

"That girl will get slapped if she gives me one more dirty look," Miracle said under her breath.

"She's just a bore," Blondie said with a shrug.

We decided to get our drinks and sit in the shaded area

underneath a tiki umbrella that was connected to the Tiki Hut.

"What's up with your security guard?" Justine asked as soon as we sat down.

"What do you mean?" I was confused as to how she knew about Maurice and me.

"You know your bodyguard, Rick," Justine said with a smile.

"Oh..." I said realizing who she was referring to.

"Rick is cool," I said simply.

"Is he single?" Justine pried raising her eyebrows.

"Don't tell me you're feeling Rick?" I said in disbelief.

"I don't know. He's cute."

"Well, as far as I know, he's single. I can't believe you're crushing on Rick!"

"How did y'all meet?" Justine inquired.

"He's staff. He works for my...for my business partner, so he's always around."

"And?"

"And what?"

"Girl, give me the juice. Is he a good guy? Does he have a lot of baby mama drama? What's his zodiac sign?" She grilled me.

"You will have to talk to him to get all that information. We just work together. How the hell would I know his sign?" I asked laughing.

"Since your relationship is strictly business, you wouldn't mind hooking us up?"

"I'm not playing cupid, Jess. If you like him, then

tell him, and I'm sure you can have him." I said before sipping my mango daiquiri.

"Now, he sounds kind of slutty," Justine said with a look of disgust. We both laughed. "Excuse me ladies, sorry to interrupt, but I was just wondering if you wanted to join us for a game of volleyball? We're two players short," A tall, dark, handsome guy asked in a deep Jamaican accent.

"I'm Madam Mi," I said offering him my hand.

"Nice to meet you. I'm Duncan and this is my friend, Charles. He motioned towards his friend who stood beside him and was holding a volleyball and smiling at Justine.

"I'm Jess," Justine offered with a big smile. Duncan flashed a perfect smile displaying a set of straight, white teeth. I realized he was still holding my hand and reluctantly pulled away.

"Sure, we'll play," I said answering for me and Justine.

"Let us just put our towels down and we'll meet you over there," I said mesmerized by his smooth, dark skin and long dreads that were pulled back.

I watched as his muscular, 6'2 frame walked away toward the volleyball court with his friend.

Justine pretended to faint on the table in an overly exaggerated motion, and I busted up laughing.

"You're crazy! Come on, let's go!" I said excitedly.

We put our towels down. I put on my orange bikini top and pulled on a pair of white short shorts over my orange bikini bottoms. Justine traded her towel for her hot pink bikini top and wrapped her sarong around her hips. We giggled like school girls on our way to catch up with the guys.

After we'd worked up a sweat playing volleyball, Duncan and I decided to get something to eat.

"So, where are you from?" Duncan asked with interest.

"California," I said eating the toppings off my pizza.

"Oh, I can see it," Duncan said playfully.

"See what?"

"California girls look, you know," he shrugged with a laugh, "like celebrities."

"I don't know about all that, but thanks I guess," I said enjoying his company.

"I'm a Cali girl with southern roots."

"How so?"

"My mama is originally from Louisiana and my daddy was born in Mississippi."

"But you, Madam, were born and raised in sunny California," he said with a smile.

"Exactly, so what about you? Where are you from?"

"I was born and raised in Kingston,"

"So, that accent is real?" I asked teasing.

"What accent?" Duncan asked with a smile.

"So, Madam, may I have your phone number?" Duncan asked looking into my eyes.

"Only if you use it," I said flirtatiously.

Duncan and I exchanged numbers and then I told him I had to meet up with my friend. Justine had headed back to the hotel over an hour ago complaining she was starting to get a headache. I knew she was just over Duncan's friend, Charles. Every chance he got he continued to flirt with anything in a bikini, and he was kind of arrogant.

When I got back to the hotel, Justine didn't answer her door and when I called her I got her voicemail, so I figured she'd decided to take a nap. I went back to my suite and took a hot shower, washing off the smell of the beach and the sand from my skin. I got out and put on my long, white terry cloth robe and flipped through the pages of the event guide that the resort provided for the tourists.

I saw that there was going to be a fire show tonight down at the beach, and I considered going if Justine was feeling up to it. I knew I could probably sell her on it if I didn't mention that there would probably be hot, steamy, shirtless, men eating flames. I laughed out loud thinking of how uptight Justine could be. She hadn't changed much since we were kids I thought shaking my head.

I slipped on a short white sundress with wedge heels and decided to do a little shopping.

On my way to the elevator, I saw Trish and Blondie.

"Hey, Madam Mi," Trish said holding a wine cooler.

"Hey, girls, where y'all going?"

"To the bar downstairs, wanna come?" Blondie asked.

"No, I wanna shop."

"I wanna go," Blondie whined.

"Okay, but let's stop by Ricks room and tell him we're leaving, so he doesn't blow a blood vessel," I said.

Trish and Blondie giggled at the thought. When I knocked on Rick's door there was no answer, so I turned to leave when he came to the door shirtless and out of breath.

"What's up Madam?"

"Nothing," I said with a puzzled expression, "I just wanted you to know that me and the girls are gonna go shopping. We'll be back in a few hours."

"Rick, come on," a female voice whined from inside his hotel room.

"Alright, see y'all later," Rick said.

As he was about to close the door, Justine appeared behind him in only her bra and panties. Blondie and Trish's mouth dropped open as Justine stood looking embarrassed.

"We'll...uhhh...see you later," I stammered before turning on my heel and rushing down the hall toward the elevator.

Blondie and Trish ran behind me laughing.

"Oh my gosh, Miss Goody-Goody is getting her swerve on with Rick!" Blondie exclaimed.

Justine told me she was feeling Rick so I wasn't too surprised, but I didn't think she would give it up so fast. I didn't want Justine to feel awkward later, but by the look on her face she was mortified.

As I was picking out new bathing suits, my cell phone rang.

"Hello?"

"Hey, Mia. How's Miami?" Coffees deep raspy voice spoke into my ear.

"Fine, how's my house?"

"Everything's going as planned."

"What's up?" I asked holding my phone tucked between my shoulder and ear as I held up different bikinis.

"I was just checking on you,'" Coffee admitted.

"I'm good, just shopping."

Coffee lingered on the phone for a little while longer before telling me to call if I needed anything and hung up. He had a way of staying relevant in my life even when I was surrounded by gorgeous, half naked men.

Justine called me when I was on my way back to my hotel

room, and we agreed to meet in my room in the next few minutes. I brought in four shopping bags full of clothes, shoes and swimsuits. I couldn't wait to try on my new outfits.

"Oh my gosh. You're gonna need another suitcase!" Justine exclaimed when she saw all my shopping bags.

"Wait until you see these new heels I bought!"

I pulled on a short, tight red dress with a plunging neckline that put my cleavage on full display.

"Wow, that's hot," Justine said nodding her approval.

"I might wear this one to dinner with Duncan," I planned, as I looked at my reflection in my full length mirror.

"He already asked you to dinner?"

"No, but he will," I said knowingly.

"What makes you so sure?" Justine asked curiously.

"Well, he asked for my number, so when he calls he'll ask to take me out. It's just how men work," I said with a shrug.

"Wouldn't you be bummed if he doesn't call?"

"He'll call. He knows I'm only in town for a couple of days, so he'll probably call tomorrow," I predicted.

"Madam Mi, you have so much confidence," Justine said as she watched me try on different outfits.

"Speaking of confidence, how did you seduce Rick so quickly?" I asked addressing the elephant in the room. Justine laughed.

"I wouldn't call it a seduction. I ran into Rick on my way back to the room, so we started talking in the elevator and I ended up getting off on his floor..."

"And?" I asked raising my eyebrows.

"And what?" Justine played coy.

"What's his sign?" We both busted up laughing.

"So, was it good?" I asked being nosey.

"It was the best twenty seconds a girl could ask for," Justine said laughing.

"Dang, poor Rick," I said shaking my head.

"What?! Poor me, I took your advice about stepping out of my comfort zone and it was just..."

I looked at Justine waiting for her to finish.

"Disappointing to put it nicely. I guess some big things do come in small packages," Justine said holding her hand up with her thumb and index finger about three inches apart.

We both laughed.

"Well, at least you didn't waste lots of time to get the same result. It's better you find out now, than to spend time getting invested, just to be disappointed later."

"Well that makes sense, but I'm still kinda feeling him."

"Really?" I asked in disbelief.

"Girl, sex ain't everything."

"I can't relate," I laughed.

"So, you mean to tell me if the sex isn't good the relationship won't work?" Justine questioned me.

"If the sex isn't good, there won't be a relationship," I said and we both cracked up laughing.

Fifteen

I woke up the next morning with a pounding headache from all the alcohol we'd drunk the night before. Justine and I had decided to go to the fire show and ended up at a bar. We were served free shots and drinks all night by a cute bartender named Chris. He flirted with me and we exchanged numbers. After the first few shots, the rest of the night was kind of a blur. I managed to make it back to my hotel room safely, but I fell asleep in all of my clothes, including my heels.

Miracle called to invite me to a breakfast buffet, but I declined. I just wanted to sleep.

My phone rang again and I answered annoyed.

"What?" I snapped.

"Good Morning, Madam. Is it a bad time?" I recognized that deep Jamaican accent immediately.

"Oh no, sorry," I said sitting up.

"How are you?" he asked sounding concerned.

"I'm great," I lied.

"How are you?"

"Great, but I only have one more night in town so I wanted to know if you were free to join me for dinner tonight?"

"You want to spend your last night in town with me? Aww, I feel so special," I said playfully.

"I would be honored to take you out, if you're feeling up to it."

"Sure," I said with a smile, enjoying the sound of Duncan's accent.

"Where are we going?"

"I'll surprise you, just meet me at the Bridge Hotel at seven."

"Okay, see you tonight," I said excitedly before hanging up.

Suddenly, I was feeling much better. I called room service to order orange juice and toast and went to take a shower. After I was showered and dressed I still had a slight headache, but I wasn't about to let that put a damper on my day.

I heard a knock at my door and figured it was my breakfast, but as I opened the door to my surprise it was Rick.

"Oh hey, what's up?" I asked

"Can I come in?" he asked with a serious tone.

"Sure." Rick rushed inside and began to nervously pace the floor.

"What's up Rick?" I asked, wondering if he knew that Justine told me the details of their quick encounter. He must have figured she would; Justine was my friend and girls talk.

"Madam Mi, sit down. We need to talk," Rick said looking as though he had a lot on his mind.

I sat at the foot of my bed, as Rick continued to pace.

"Rick, what the hell is going on?" I demanded growing impatient.

"Coffee got picked up this morning," Rick blurted out.

"What?" I exclaimed.

"Why?! What happened? Is he..."

Rick cut me off before I could finish my line of questioning.

"I don't have the details, I just know he's been picked up because I got the text."

"What text?"

"One of our men notified the crew by sending a coded text message," Rick explained.

"Well maybe you misunderstood the code."

"I didn't. He was picked up, but maybe he was only brought in for questioning,"

"Coffee's smart. He knows not to talk without an attorney," I said attempting to calm my nerves.

"Yeah," Rick agreed but he still looked worried.

"What are you not telling me?"

"Coffee would like to keep the details of his business affairs private, so if anything ever happened you wouldn't be considered an accomplice."

"So, is that a nice way of telling me it's none of my business?" I asked crossing my arms.

There was a knock on the door and for a second I thought I saw Rick freeze from fear as he looked at the door.

"It's probably my breakfast," I said getting up and looking through the peephole.

I opened the door, and the bellhop rolled in a cart with a full breakfast spread of toast, jam, butter, and honey, a pitcher of orange juice and an assortment of fresh fruit.

"Thanks," I said giving him a tip before he left. I went back to sit on the bed. Suddenly I didn't have an appetite.

"Look, Rick. I know Coffee is your boss, so you have to take his orders seriously. I can respect that, but whatever Coffee is keeping from me, I'm already tied to. I'm his business partner, and the reason we're out here in Florida is because Coffee's operation is being investigated. An operation that he ran out of my house! So please! Skip the part about keeping me safe and just tell me what I'm up against," I demanded.

"Alright," Ricked sighed and looked a little relieved. "Somebody is talking to the police. We keep a real low profile, so it looks like the police's informant is one of our own," Rick said shaking his head.

"Coffee's not even sure who to trust. I know Coffee won't crack inside an interrogation room, but if this snitch is talking, it's only a matter of time until people's names are dropped and they start getting called in for questioning."

I sat in silence for a few moments processing everything Rick had said.

"Does Coffee have any leads on who the rat might be?"

"At first, he figured it was some of Barlow's crew, because he had what you might call a disagreement with a few of them over business. They were close to our operation, and they had some classified information. When we moved the operation out of your garage to the new spot, no one outside of our crew knew about the move. So, whoever put the police onto the new spot has to be someone in the crew".

"So, doesn't that narrow it down?" I asked

"We have a large staff," Rick said vaguely.

My phone rang and I answered it quickly, hoping to hear Coffee's voice.

"Hello? Hey girl, you already up? Last night was so fun!

What do you got planned for today?" Justine asked through the phone.

"Oh hey, Jess. I'm just getting ready for the day, I'll come to your room in a minute," I said rushing her off the phone.

"Don't bother. I'm already outside your door. I figured I'd come wake you up from your hangover." She tapped on the outside of the hotel door.

I hung up.

"It's Justine," I told Rick.

"Madam Mi, I know I don't have to tell you not to share this information with anyone," Rick said questioningly.

"Yeah, I know."

"Also, we don't know whose phone lines are tapped so don't talk business over the phone. When Coffee contacts you just tell him, 'We all met at the same restaurant,' and he'll know you've been caught up to speed," Rick explained before opening the hotel door and walking passed Justine without another word.

"What the hell was that about?" Justine asked with her eyebrows raised, crossing her arms in front of her chest.

"Rick is just mad that I got so drunk last night, and he didn't know where I was. Since he's my security, I guess I got him in trouble with his boss," I lied.

Justine didn't look convinced.

"I thought you were just waking up." She looked at the breakfast cart in the middle of the room.

"Yeah, I figured toast and orange juice would cure my hangover."

"Madam Mi, are you sleeping with Rick?" Justine asked accusingly.

"What?" I snapped.

"I mean why else would he be in your room this early? And you clearly didn't just wake up. Your hair is still wet from your shower and you're fully dressed!"

"Why the hell would I ever sleep with Rick?" I asked with a laugh.

"I don't do miniature quickies," I said harshly.

"Trust me, Jess, he's all yours. Rick and I only have a business relationship."

"Somehow, I find that a little hard to believe," Justine snapped before turning and walking out.

I had too much on my mind to care about Justine's illusions. I was worried about Coffee and concerned about what all this meant for me. If somebody was a threat to Coffee's freedom, then ultimately, they were a threat to mine. By the look on Rick's face, that threat was very real. I didn't know many of the guys Coffee employed as staff, but the ones I knew seemed very loyal, and I couldn't imagine them being an informant to the police. I just wished Coffee allowed me more access to his end of the business. Then, I would be able to wrap my head around all this a little better. He did a good job of shutting me out. I was lucky to have gotten the information I'd gotten from Rick, even though it wasn't much.

I decided to take advantage of a massage at the resort's Day Spa. I figured it would help me relax; I felt so tense. Before I called to book an appointment, there was a knock at the door. I looked through the peephole and saw Blondie and Miracle. I opened the door not really feeling like company.

"Madam Mi, you shoulda came to breakfast. It was so good!" Miracle smiled.

"Yeah, I'm stuffed," Blondie agreed.

"I didn't feel up to it. Where are the other girls?"

"Erica is probably still puking her brains out. That girl can't hold her liquor," Blondie said shaking her head.

"What about Trish?"

"She went with us to the club last night too, and she didn't wanna get up," Miracle said.

"I wanna go down to the beach and work on my tan," Blondie said flipping her hair.

"What you got planned?" Miracle asked.

"Where's Miss Prissy?" Blondie asked referring to Justine.

"I don't know, she'll probably meet up with me later," I shrugged.

"I think I'll get a massage at that Day Spa,"

"Oh I wanna go," Blondie whined.

"I want a mud bath," Miracle said.

"I heard the spa has a sauna and when you get all sweaty, it burns off like calories and stuff," Blondie said picking the grapes out of my fruit bowl. Miracle and I both laughed.

"What?" Blondie asked obliviously.

My thirty-minute massage was just what I needed. The scented oils that the masseuse massaged into my skin relaxed every muscle in my body. As I got all the kinks rubbed out of my neck, I decided I should get a massage at least once a week. It was so relaxing. Afterward, I met up with Blondie and Miracle in the sauna. When I entered the steamy room, they were wrapped in their white towels talking in low voices. When they saw me, they stopped talking.

"What's up?" I asked curiously.

"Nothing," Miracle said unconvincingly.

I sat down on the hard, wooden bench.

"Why do I feel like there's an elephant in the room?"

"How would an elephant fit in here?" Blondie asked looking around the small wooden sauna.

"I mean there seems to be something that needs to be discussed, but it's not being said," I clarified, and Miracle rolled her eyes at Blondie's ignorance.

"Oh..." Blondie said.

"So what are you not telling me?" I asked, looking from Blondie to Miracle for an answer.

"Nothing, Madam Mi. Miracle was just saying that Brandy told Destiny that Coffee went to jail this morning and she was wondering if you knew about it," Blondie confessed.

Miracle shot Blondie a dirty look and rolled her eyes.

"Madam Mi, we weren't trying to be in your business. I only brought it up because my sister called and..." I interrupted Miracles explanation as I got up from the wooden bench.

"You can tell your sister to stop gossiping! I know exactly where Coffee is and it's really none of her concern," I said before opening the foggy glass door and walking out.

When I got out of the shower, I had three missed calls from Justine. Before I could get dressed there was a knock at my door. I pulled on my robe and let Justine in.

"Hey, girl, bad time?" She asked as she glanced around the room.

"Come on in. Rick and I have already finished having wild, crazy sex," I said sarcastically.

Justine came in and rolled her eyes.

"Very funny, Madam Mi. Look, I'm sorry about earlier. I didn't mean to accuse you of sleeping with Rick."

"Oh really? Because it seemed to me like you had your mind made up," I said with an attitude.

"I know, I'm sorry. It's just that I feel he's been ignoring me, and then when I saw him, he practically ran out of here this morning not even acknowledging me. I just let my assumptions get the best of me."

"Okay, apology accepted," I said, happy Justine had come to her senses.

"You guys haven't talked?" I asked.

"Nope, he just acts too busy and you know what? I get it. Maybe it wasn't the best decision to sleep with Rick before I even knew his last name."

"Maybe he's embarrassed about that quick ass performance," I suggested.

Justine looked hurt.

"I'm serious, girl. I think he just lost all respect for me," Justine said sinking down on my bed.

"Jess, get it together. Did you ever consider that he really is just busy?" I asked attempting to cheer her up.

"You think?" Justine asked curiously.

"Well, I know Rick, and it seems like he's been a little on edge. I mean you seen how he stormed out of here earlier."

"Did he mention anything about me?"

"Nope, just business. Rick is under a lot of pressure at his job."

"So, what do you think I should do?"

"Nothing. Just chill, and have a good time in Miami. Let him come to you."

"You're right. I'm done texting and calling him."

I was relieved to hear Justine come to that conclusion, because I knew Rick was dealing with a much bigger problem, and Justine was kind of clingy.

"What do we have planned tonight?" Justine asked.

"I told you I have a date with Duncan," I reminded her.

"So, he called?" Justine asked with surprise.

I rolled my eyes.

"Yeah, girl. I told you I know how guys work."

"So where is he taking you?"

"Just to dinner, but I'm anticipating dessert," I said with a laugh.

"Oh my gosh, are you gonna sleep with him tonight?"

"I don't know, if the chemistry is right. Tonight's his last night in town."

"Well, have fun," Justine said shaking her head.

"Too bad you weren't feeling Charles. We could have gone on a double date."

"Girl, please! He was so self-absorbed," Justine said rolling her eyes.

I couldn't help but laugh.

"He wasn't even that cute. But Duncan....he's fine!"

"I know!" I squealed with excitement.

Sixteen

That night I had mixed feelings about going out with Duncan. I still hadn't heard from Coffee, and no matter how hard I tried to push him out of my mind, he kept creeping back inside my thoughts. I was determined to have a good time with Duncan despite the nagging feeling of concern I had for Coffee. I decided against the red dress and chose a long sleeved, black mini dress with a plunging neckline that stopped just above my navel. I wore gold accessories and leopard print pumps. I wore my hair down, curled in ringlet spirals. I knew I was looking good.

I waited downstairs in the lobby of the Bridge Hotel for ten minutes, until finally, the elevator doors opened. Duncan got off holding a bouquet of white orchids. He was wearing a crisp white collared shirt and a black suit. He looked very handsome. A few women in the hotel lobby stopped and stared enviously as Duncan flashed his perfect, white smile and walked towards me.

"Hello, Beautiful. I'm sorry I'm late," he apologized as he handed me my flowers and kissed my cheek. He smelled delicious. His cologne and the smell of his aftershave made my knees weak. I smiled, trying to calm my nerves.

"No problem," I managed to say.

Duncan had made reservations at the Lantern; it was an upscale restaurant that overlooked the beach. We were seated on the balcony and served wine, while we looked over our menus.

"I hope you enjoy seafood," Duncan said before tasting his wine.

"Sometimes," I said looking over the menu.

"I think I know what you may like," Duncan said with a smile.

"Really? What's that?"

"How about the shrimp and crab salad?"

"Sounds good," I said putting my menu down.

I wasn't use to a man ordering for me, or even offering to. I enjoyed how Duncan was a take-charge-kind-of-guy. He ordered the surf and turf for himself and when our plates came, he offered me a piece of his steak from his fork. I leaned in and allowed Duncan to feed me.

"Mmm, that's really good," I said.

"I would let you taste mine, but I don't share my food," I said playfully.

We both laughed.

"So why is tonight your last night in town?" I asked enjoying his company.

"I have to get back to work,"

"What do you do?" I asked.

"I'm a personal trainer."

"Oh, that makes sense," I said looking over his muscular physique.

"What about yourself?"

"I run a business," I answered vaguely.

"Oh, you're a businesswoman," Duncan said impressed.

"What kind of business?"

"I manage an adult escort service." Duncan nodded as he processed what I had just said.

"So, you're a pimp?" he asked with a laugh.

"I'm a Madam," I corrected.

"Wow, that's sexy."

"Well, thank you," I said sipping my wine.

"When I leave, can we keep in touch?"

"You have my number," I said with a smile.

"You are very beautiful, Madam Mi," Duncan complimented me.

"I only wish I hadn't met you at the end of my vacation, so we could have spent more time together,"

"We will just have to make the most of tonight," I said flirtatiously.

He lifted his wine glass in agreement and I lifted mine allowing them to touch. We both drank.

After dinner, Duncan declined dessert and paid our bill. He asked me if I wanted to walk with him on the beach. I took off my heels and we both walked barefoot in the soft, thick sand holding hands.

"I should have brought my bikini," I said with a laugh.

"You would swim?"

"No, I'm just kidding, it's probably too cold," I admitted.

"You're no fun," Duncan teased.

"I dare you to," I challenged.

"Right now?"

"Unless you're scared!"

"I'll go, if you go with me."

"I'm too chicken," I laughed.

"Come on, now you got me willing to," he said as he stopped walking and began unbuttoning his shirt.

"Are you going to go naked?" I asked raising my eyebrows.

"Yeah, why not?" he asked casually.

"Okay, let's do it!"

"Really?" Duncan asked with a smile.

I dropped my heels and pulled my dress over my head. I ran towards the water wearing only my bra and panties. Duncan followed my lead and stripped down to his boxers and chased me into the water. To my surprise the water was warm.

"It's not cold," I said with surprise.

Duncan pulled me towards him and embraced my body with his strong arms. He held me close to his chest and I looked up at him. The warm waves splashed against our bodies and he began to kiss me as I stood wrapped in his strong muscular arms. I enjoyed the feel of his soft, thick lips and returned his kiss allowing his tongue to enter my mouth and dance with my own. He led and I followed. Our lips were in sync and I began to feel warm all over.

Duncan lifted me up and carried me back to shore. I draped my arms around his shoulders, enjoying the feeling of being rescued. Once he placed my feet down on the sand, I picked up my belongings and ran ahead of him, laughing as he chased behind me. He caught up, grabbing me by my waist and held me in a bear hug from behind.

"Let's go back to the hotel," he whispered in my ear.

When we got back to the Bridge Hotel, I was holding my dress and purse and wearing Duncan's suit coat with my heels. Duncan looked disheveled in his wrinkled suit. We ignored the stares we got from the people in the lobby and took the elevator upstairs.

****

The next morning I had to do the walk of shame back to my hotel. I picked up my flowers from the front desk and made my way through the lobby and to the outdoors, ignoring the judgmental stares from the nosey onlookers. When I got to my room I kicked off my heels and collapsed on my bed, reminiscing about my night with Duncan. I could still smell his cologne on my skin and I was in no rush to shower. I drifted off to sleep thinking of Duncan.

I was pulled from my dream by the ringing of my cell phone.

"Hello?" I mumbled half asleep.

"Mia, you up?" A deep raspy voice asked through the phone.

I sat up and was suddenly wide awake.

"Coffee!" I exclaimed, happy to hear from him.

"How's Miami?" Coffee asked casually.

I wanted to ask a million questions, but I knew I couldn't ask them over the phone.

"It's fine," I answered trying to remember the phrase Rick told me to use so Coffee would know that he'd told me about the snitch. My head was still foggy from just waking up and I couldn't recall what Rick had said.

"Are you okay?" I asked concerned.

"Yeah, I'm straight."

"So, I'll be home in a few days," I said. My statement sounded more like a question than a comment.

"Okay, I'll see you when you get back."

"Alright."

"I was just checking on you," Coffee said getting ready to hang up.

"We all met at the same restaurant," I said remembering the code.

"Yeah, I know," Coffee said before he said goodbye and hung up.

Seventeen

It felt good to be back at home. I missed my house, my bed and my Bentley. The working girls seemed to have enjoyed their vacation also. They were in much better spirits, and there was less bickering. Justine and I became very close. We drank up the Miami sunshine and partied every night as though it were our last. I ended up hooking Justine up with the cute, blonde, bartender named Chris, and they'd really hit it off. I was glad Justine had a little fling outside of her obsession with Rick, because he didn't seem interested in having any kind of relationship with her.

I'd been home for three weeks, and I still hadn't seen Coffee. He'd sent me a bouquet of welcome home flowers the day we got back, but they were delivered by a flower delivery company. It was a nice gesture but impersonal.

The card in the flowers was typed and read,

"Welcome Home. –Coffee". When I called him, I got his voicemail.

A few hours later, he texted me saying, "I'm a little busy, but what's up?"

I was annoyed by his distance, but decided to focus my attention on my own business affairs.

I was ready to accept more girls in the house. I'd come

to terms with Brandy and Coffee's betrayal and decided that I wasn't going to allow my emotions to hinder my finances. I wasn't just going to hire any random set of girls, but they would have to come with a credible reference to be considered. Blondie referred her friend, Lexi, and Trish referred Layla. Both girls were living in the house on probationary terms, and I paid close attention to their work ethic and earnings.

Lexi had bleach blonde hair and blue eyes like Blondie, but she seemed to be a lot smarter. She hadn't been in the business long, but she had experience as a stripper and she wasn't shy. Layla was short and chubby, but she made double what the other girls could in one night. She had a smooth, chocolate complexion and instead of hair extensions like the other girls wore, she wore her hair gelled back into a donut-style bun. Layla called Trish "Sis," because they were raised by the same foster care mother. I liked that she didn't get caught up in other girls petty arguing but focused on her money. Business was good on my end, and I assumed the same could be said about Coffee's situation. Since I'd been back, I hadn't heard anything about a continued investigation.

Rick had been reassigned to work alongside Coffee. Maurice and Tony were left to provide security outside my house. I didn't know Tony well, but I'd seen him enough times to know Coffee trusted him. I figured the snitch had been caught and the threat was in the past.

As soon as I'd gotten back home, Maurice and I picked up our secret sexual relationship where we'd left off. There was something exhilarating about sneaking around. We'd come dangerously close to being caught a few times, but that had only increased the thrill of it all. Of course, we could have kept our sex escapades behind closed doors, but that was just too safe and boring. Instead, we opted for the kitchen countertops, outside in the Jacuzzi, and my personal favorite, against any wall in the house. We were friends with benefit and had no romantic connection.

"Madam Mi, how much longer do you want to keep this up?" Maurice asked as he pulled up his Levi's and buckled his belt.

"What do you mean? "I asked, jumping down from the kitchen countertop, adjusting my dress.

"So, you would prefer for us to keep sneaking around?"

"I thought you were concerned about keeping your job."

"I don't think Coffee will be a threat to our relationship much longer," Maurice said confidently.

"What do you mean, Maurice?"

"Nothing you need to worry your pretty little head about," He said, kissing me on my forehead.

"Maurice, you know Coffee is not the kind of person who will forgive if he's betrayed," I warned.

"But you are?" he asked shaking his head.

"What do you mean?" I asked crossing my arms.

"You forgave him when he betrayed you, and you're still willing to work for him."

"I don't work for him. We are business partners, and our relationship isn't personal. It's strictly business," I said defensively.

"Maurice if you're planning to get rid of Coffee, I need to know about it because it affects my business."

"Madam Mi, you deserve a partner you can trust, and I think we will make a great team," Maurice said leaning in and kissing my lips.

"Why do I get the feeling that you already have your mind made up about this?"

"I would be lying if I didn't say my mind has been made up for a while. This isn't some spur of the moment plan. I've been sitting back and waiting patiently for the opportunity for my takeover and now that it's happening, I know that I'm ready for this. I didn't expect to fall in love with you, but now I see you as part of the plan. We could build an empire together, just you and me.

"What's your plan for this takeover?" I pried.

"You don't have to worry about the details. I just need to know that you're on my side. I need to know that when it's all said and done, you're gonna be my partner, my chick," Maurice said searching my face for answers.

"Maurice I didn't know you felt this way about me," I said trying to gather my thoughts.

"I've been risking my life to be with you, and it's not just about sex. I've fallen in love with you Madam Mi," Maurice said putting his hands on my hips and looking me in the eyes.

"I..."

Just then Tony opened the front door,

"Maurice, Boss is on the phone," he called out.

"Alright, here I come," Maurice yelled back.

He kissed me and left the house. It was all too surreal. I couldn't believe what I'd heard.

Maurice had fallen in love with me! And more importantly, Maurice was the rat!

Eighteen

"Too bad I missed the big vacay. Sounds like fun!" Lexi said as she straightened her extensions.

"It was! Madam Mi knows how to have a good time!" Blondie bragged.

"You gotta prove yourself, Chica, if you expect to travel and lay up for a week in the sun," Erica interjected.

"I can't afford to miss a week of work. I have responsibilities to take care of," Layla said while doing her makeup.

"You would turn down an all-expense paid trip?" Lexi asked unconvinced.

"I'm here to work, not party."

"Well, Chica, aren't you the over achiever," Erica said sarcastically while rolling her eyes.

"Oh my gosh, Erica. Why do you bitch about them proving themselves and then bug when they're serious about making money? There's no pleasing you," Blondie snapped.

"Well, it's a good thing I'm not here to please..her," Layla retorted before getting up and walking out of the makeup room.

Lexi laughed as she continued to do her hair.

"I'm just sick of all these new Chicas thinking they can just come in here and take over," Erica complained before turning and storming out of the room.

"Wow, someone has serious PMS," Lexi said.

She and Blondie cracked up laughing.

****

While the girls were upstairs getting dressed to go out to work, I decided to try Coffee's cell phone again. I'd been getting his voicemail all day. I planned to tell Coffee what Maurice was up to, but I knew it was a conversation we had to have in person, and it had to be sooner rather than later. I didn't know Maurice's timeline. In the meantime, I would have to pretend that Maurice and I were on the same page. I didn't want to tell Coffee the details of our secret affair, but I knew it might have to come out if I were going to explain the seriousness of Maurice's threat. Coffee's life was in danger.

I was happy when the girls were ready to go out. Maurice and Tony took turns escorting them to the track, while the other one stayed behind to provide security. Since Maurice had stayed behind last night, I knew he'd be taking the girls tonight. I was relieved that he would be out of my hair for a few hours. If only I could get a hold of Coffee while they were gone.

"Madam Mi, we'll see you later," Trish said as her high heels clicked across the floor breaking my train of thought.

"Okay," I said watching the last few girls rush downstairs and head for the door. They had faces full of makeup, wearing very little clothes paired with high heels. Before I could get up to lock the door, the doorknob turned and in walked Coffee. I froze, feeling relief, surprise and then anger when I noticed he was holding onto the hand of an attractive, caramel-com-plexioned woman.

"Hey, Mia," Coffee said casually.

I glared at Coffee and then turned my attention towards the female that had the nerve to come into my home, holding Coffee's hand and smiling like it were acceptable.

"Who's this?" I asked looking her over.

"Mia, this is my girlfriend, Tiffany. Tiffany, this is my business partner, Mia," Coffee introduced us with a smile on his face.

Tiffany extended her hand.

"Hello, Mia, I've heard so much about you," she said po-litely.

"I can't say the same," I said shaking her hand. Tiffany's smile faded as I shot Coffee a dirty look.

"We need to talk," I said turning and walking towards the kitchen.

Coffee began to follow me, still holding onto Tiffany's hand. "It's business," I said coldly.

"I can wait in the living room," she suggested.

"That would be ideal," I said rudely.

"So, what's up?" Coffee asked as Tiffany walked back to-wards the living room.

"Coffee, why are you bringing females to my house?" I de-manded folding my arms across my chest.

"What are you talking about, Mia?" Coffee asked inno-cently.

"So, you think it's okay to bring your little girlfriends over here and flaunt them in my face?" I was upset!

"Look, Mia, I didn't mean to flaunt anybody in your face. We were on our way out and since I was passing through the neighborhood, I figured I'd swing by and let you meet Tiffany."

"I've been calling you all day," I said frustrated.

"Yeah, I've been a little busy. I'm here now, so what's up?" Coffee asked nonchalantly.

"Coffee, we're running a business together, so it's important that I'm able to communicate with you!"

"Okay, I can understand that. So again, Mia, what's up?" Coffee asked impatiently.

"Babe, I don't mean to interrupt, but if we're going to make the movie, we should really get going," Tiffany said as she poked her head into the kitchen.

"Look, Tiffany, Coffee is a business man. He has to take care of business, which happens to be more important than your little movie date," I said condescending.

"I didn't mean to..." Tiffany began.

"Babe, I'll be right there just give me a minute," Coffee said calmly.

"Okay, Babe," Tiffany said going back to the living room.

Coffee turned his attention back towards me with his jaw clenched tight as though he were angry.

"I don't know what the hell is wrong with you, Mia, but I'm not going to allow you to be rude to her when she's done nothing to you. If you want to discuss business, I will be here tomorrow morning. Right now, I'm running late. I gotta go,"

Coffee said turning and walking out of the house holding Tiffany's hand.

"Nice meeting you," Tiffany said politely looking at me over her shoulder as they walked out and closed the door.

I was furious.

Coffee had a lot of nerve, bringing that woman into my house and acting as if I were out of line when clearly his intentions were to make me jealous. I had been worried about his well-being and he was off setting up movie dates and cruising around town as though he didn't have a care in the world. Since he had no regard for my feelings, I wouldn't try to spare his. He was in for a rude awakening tomorrow at our business meeting.

I'd managed to steer clear of Maurice since his confession in the kitchen. I guess he was tied up with work because I hadn't received a text or phone call. I saw this as a blessing and a curse. On one hand, I wouldn't have to keep up a facade of being in love with him, but if he were busy at work, I was kept out of the loop. I was concerned for Coffee's safety. I didn't know what he was planning.

The next morning, I woke up and decided this time I would not allow Coffee to leave without knowing exactly what was going on. I only hoped he wouldn't bring that pageant-queen-look-alike Tiffany along.

As I got dressed in a short, tight, white pencil skirt and black button down blouse, I looked in the mirror at my curves and wondered what the hell Coffee could possibly see in her. I had my highlighted hair extensions taken out after Miami, and I now wore my hair jet black, slicked back into a ponytail that reached the end of my back. After I finished my makeup I stepped into my black stilettos and headed downstairs, ready for my business meeting.

The doorbell rang. When I opened the door, I was surprised to see Justine.

"Hey Jess," I said allowing her inside.

"Hey girl, you look nice," Justine said admiring my outfit.

"Thanks, I have a meeting in a few."

"So, you're back to business," Justine sounded disappointed.

"When's the next time we're gonna hang out?"

"I don't know, I've been pretty busy."

"Okay, well just call me soon, so we can make plans to go out. I gotta get going, I'm on my way to the shop."

"When you dropped by, were you hoping to run into Rick?" I asked knowingly.

"Maybe," Justine admitted with a smile.

"I haven't seen him lately, but when I do I'll let him know he has a stalker," I teased.

"You better not!" Justine laughed.

"Alright, I gotta go! Call me," Justine said rushing off to work.

I wanted to confide in her about Coffee and his new girlfriend, but then I would have to explain the extent of our relationship and I didn't want to dive back into that pool of emotions.

****

When Coffee finally arrived at the house, I was glad to see he'd come alone.

"You're late," I pointed out as Coffee let himself in.

"I'm a busy man."

"Let's go upstairs."

Coffee smiled.

"We have to discuss business and it's serious," I said walking ahead of Coffee allowing his eyes to take in the full view of my feminine figure as he followed me up the stairs and into my bedroom.

"So, what's up?" Coffee asked as soon as he closed the door.

"I found the rat," I said cutting straight to the chase.

"What do you mean?" Coffee asked with a puzzled expression.

"When you got locked up while I was in Florida, Rick told me that you suspected one of your own was working as an informant for the cops."

Coffee nodded.

"And?"

"After I got back, I found out that the snitch is Maurice," I said in a hushed voice.

"I know you trust him and..."

"Who told you this?" Coffee asked curiously.

"He did."

"Maurice came to you and said he was working as an informant for the police?" Coffee asked unconvinced.

"Well, not exactly,"

"Mia, tell me exactly what was said," Coffee said taking my hand and pulling me to sit beside him at the foot of my bed.

"Maurice told me he was planning to take over your company. He said you wouldn't pose a problem for him much longer, and that he'd been patiently waiting for his opportunity and now he's ready to take it."

"I see, and why didn't you tell me?"

"I've been trying to, but you have been too occupied with your little girlfriend to see the threat your own staff poses to you!"

"I have everything under control," Coffee assured me.

"So, you knew about Maurice?!" I asked with surprise.

"Yeah, and I told you I didn't want you involved in my end of the business!"

"What? Why would you keep Maurice around if you knew he was a snitch all this time?" I asked confused.

"Haven't you ever heard the saying, 'Keep your friends close, but your enemies closer'?"

"So, what are you going to do?"

"Do about what?"

"About Maurice! You have to get rid of him, Coffee. He can't continue to work security outside my house!" I said panicking.

"Why not? Are you done sleeping with him?" Coffee asked calmly.

I felt my heart skip a beat. I was shocked that Coffee knew about my affair with Maurice.

"Why do you look so surprised, Mia? You couldn't have possibly thought you could have sex with a member of my staff, sneaking him in and out of the house, having sex outside in the Jacuzzi and I wouldn't find out about it. Come on, Mia, you two have been hooking up for months."

"I..." I stammered.

"Don't worry about explaining anything to me. What you do in your personal life is your business. You don't have to worry about Maurice either. I'm taking care of the situation." Coffee said standing up.

"Coffee, wait," I said before he could leave.

"What?" Coffee asked with his hand on the doorknob.

"How did you know about Maurice?"

"I didn't become the boss of a million-dollar drug ring overnight. It's my nature to stay ten steps ahead at all times. I hope you will stay out of my end of the business from here on out,"

He let himself out, as I sat at the end of my bed dumbfounded.

Nineteen

Six months later, I received word that Grandma Trudy wasn't doing well. She'd been hospitalized and Mama told me she wasn't expected to live much longer. Tati had been staying with Sister Grace from the church, but she was an elderly woman and could only keep Tati temporarily. As soon as I heard, I sent for Tati and made arrangements for her to come live with me. I ordered her bedroom furniture and filled her chest of drawers and closet with new clothes.

When I went back home to visit with Grandma Trudy, she'd given me her blessing to take Tati. She told me where I could find her birth certificate and shot records, so I could register Tati at Sundown Valley Elementary School. I sat with Grandma Trudy for hours, holding her hand and talking to her as she slipped in and out of consciousness. It scared me to hear her talk about not being afraid, but ready to go. I didn't like hearing her say such things, but it made it easier to believe she would be in a better place.

When I returned the following morning, the nurse informed me that Grandma Trudy had passed away during the night.

Her funeral service was held two weeks later. I attended with Tati, dressed in white from head to toe as Grandma

Trudy had requested. She wanted all her guests to pay their respects by wearing white for her "Homecoming Ceremony" as she called it, and without tears. She wanted her passing to be a joyous occasion and her life to be celebrated as opposed to her death being mourned.

She had a small service. Her church's choir sang a few hymns while dressed in long, white choir robes and white doves were released as her coffin was lowered into the ground. It was beautiful and sad all at the same time. Tati cried a little, and we left immediately after the service. Mama told me a funeral was no place for a child, but Grandma Trudy had made it clear in her last will and testament that she wanted Tati to attend, so I honored her wishes.

Tati adjusted well to her new life in Sundown Valley. She was in the third grade and she had more than enough extracurricular activities to keep her busy when she wasn't in school. I'd enrolled her in tap dance and ballet class on Mondays and Wednesdays, piano lessons Tuesdays and Thursdays, and tennis lessons on the weekends. I had to hire a nanny to care for Tati when she wasn't in school and to help her with her homework. Her nanny was a young blonde named Annabelle who had experience as a kindergarten teacher. She had lost her teaching job after the state budget cuts. She came highly recommended by one of Shelly's friends from the shop. Tati called her Anna Banana. I was happy to have someone I could trust taking care of Tati when I wasn't around. Annabelle was patient and worked well with Tati's hyper personality.

"Mami, where you going to?" Tati asked watching me do my makeup.

"Out," I answered vaguely.

"Are you going on a date?"

"Maybe," I said applying my mascara.

"Oooh," Tati teased excitedly.

At least one of us was excited. I was going on more of a business date rather than a romantic one.

I was meeting up with Coffee at Laughlin's Lounge to discuss business. It was Coffee's idea to meet up in a public place, but I was sure the idea had really come from that overbearing little Barbie doll, Tiffany. My relationship with Coffee had been strained ever since the whole ordeal with Maurice, and his nosey girlfriend didn't make the situation any better.

She knew Coffee and I had a history together, and I think she was intimidated by me. Tiffany was all smiles whenever I saw her. She'd follow Coffee around like a little puppy dog, so I knew she had a lot of insecurities.

When I arrived at the lounge, Coffee was already there, and he looked happy to see me.

"Hello, Mia, can I get you a drink?" he asked, as I sat across from him at a small booth.

"No, thanks."

"I wanted to catch you up to speed on what my plans are for the business," Coffee said, pausing to take a drink from his glass.

"I'm going to need access to the garage again."

"That shouldn't be a problem. As long as all your guys use the back exit to enter and leave through the garage, that's fine," I shrugged.

"Good, I'll also have a few extra guys on the premises to make sure my operation is being run smoothly."

"Okay, as long as it's all done very low key. I told you I have custody of Tati, and I don't want too many strange men on my property," I reminded him.

"Just look at it like extra security."

"Alright."

"How's business going?"

Before I could answer his question, Tiffany appeared with a smile on her face holding her clutch purse underneath her arm and wearing a knee-length pink dress.

"Hello, Mia," she said all bubbly and then directed her attention towards Coffee.

"Sorry I took so long, Babe. There's practically a line in the ladies room just to get to the mirror," she explained with a giggle.

Coffee slid out of the booth and allowed Tiffany to sit on the inside. Before Coffee sat back down he flashed me a look that I took to mean "be nice." I returned his warning glare with a fake smile.

"Hello, Tiffany," I said mocking her upbeat enthusiasm.

"I only allow a select few to call me Mia, pretty much just my Mama and your man. The rest of the world refers to me as 'Madam Mi,'" I corrected her.

"Oh, I didn't mean to offend you," Tiffany said apologetically.

"None taken," I said with a wave of my hand to dismiss the conversation.

"Okay, let's get back to business," Coffee interjected, rubbing his palms together.

I raised my eyebrows wondering how we could discuss business, since Coffee had brought his sidekick along.

"Mia, Tiffany is going to join the business," Coffee said with a straight face.

"Excuse me? She hardly looks like a working girl," I said looking her over.

"Tiffany will not be working for you. She will be working for me."

I laughed as Tiffany sat there with her stupid smile plastered on her face.

"Coffee what are you talking about?" I was annoyed.

"Mia, don't get upset. I'm doing what is best for the business." He took another sip from his glass.

"You will still be running your end of the business and Tiffany will be an asset to my end."

"How so? What is it that you do?" I asked turning my attention towards Tiffany.

"I'm a pharmacy tech. I'm currently enrolled at SVU working on my degree to become a pharmacist," Tiffany said smugly.

"Wow, good for you," I said rolling my eyes.

"She doesn't have to explain to you how she's qualified to do her job," Coffee defended Tiffany.

"No, she doesn't, and since she is just a member of your staff on your end of the business, there's really no reason for her to attend our business meetings," I snapped.

"Whoa, I didn't mean to intrude," Tiffany said as though her feelings were hurt.

"Is there anything else?" I asked as I scooted off the booth seat and grabbed my purse.

Coffee looked as though he had something he wanted to say, but instead he just shook his head.

I turned and walked out of the lounge.

Twenty

Coffee had lost his mind if he thought I was going to allow him to push his little girlfriend into our business. However, on the other hand it, was comforting to know that he didn't mind involving Tiffany in his end of the business. That would mean that he must not be too emotionally involved with her if he was okay with her working inside his drug operation. Coffee was adamant about keeping me uninvolved in the details of his business for my own safety. I figured he saw her more as an opportunity to further his business rather than a serious love interest.

I'd attempted to move on emotionally from Coffee. I'd been on several dates and engaged in phone and text conversations with several different men, but none of them had kept my interest. Even Duncan had kept in touch, but I wasn't interested in a long-distance relationship. I would sit across the table from a handsome, successful man at a nice restaurant, and I would wonder if Coffee planned to come by and if he'd come alone.

As much as I hated to admit it, Tiffany posed a problem for me as far as me reconnecting with Coffee. She was a constant annoyance for me. I knew if I were going to get Coffee back, she would have to be out of the picture. I took a play from Coffee's playbook and decided to keep my friends close but my enemies closer. I called Tiffany up and convinced her to meet up with me.

"Just us girls, Tiff. I really just want to clear the air so there's no bad blood between us," I lied through the receiver.

"Really?" Tiffany asked with surprise.

"Yeah, girl. I think we got off on the wrong foot," I said convincingly.

"Okay, sounds good."

"Let's meet at the plaza in an hour,"

"Sure, Mia, I mean, Madam Mi," Tiffany corrected herself.

Annabelle wouldn't be here for another two hours, so I had to take Tati along. Having Tati with me was a good idea anyway, because I wouldn't lose my composure and accidentally slap Tiffany's stupid smile off her face in front of Tati.

"Can we get an ice cream?" Tati asked as soon as we got to the plaza.

"Yeah, you want a cone?" I asked her walking towards The Scoop.

"Yup," Tati said with excitement.

I texted Tiffany and told her to meet me at the ice cream parlor. When she arrived, Tati was eating her strawberry ice cream and talking nonstop about why her friend Emily had gotten in trouble during class.

"Hey, Madam Mi," Tiffany said with her big pageant smile.

"Hi, Tiff," I said, standing and giving her a half-hearted hug.

"This is my goddaughter, Tati,"

Tati looked Tiffany over. She said, "Hi," before going back to her cone.

"I'm glad you could make it, Tiff," I said as she took a seat with us at the small table.

"I must say, I was pretty surprised when you called. How did you get my cell phone number?"

"From Coffee," I lied.

I'd actually had to do some digging. I'd gotten her number from Shelly's receptionist because Tiffany frequented the shop to get her hair pressed, so her contact information was on file.

"Look, Tiff, if we are going to work together in the same business, then it's important that we get along. We're partners," I said with a smile.

Tiffany looked relieved.

"I was wrong the other night for storming out when Coffee said you would be a part of the business," I admitted apologetically.

"It's okay. I know it will probably just take some time to get used to the idea," Tiffany said looking pleased.

"I'm just overly protective when it comes to my baby."

Tiffany raised her eyebrows.

"You know, the business. Coffee and I have been working together for a while and we've had a few hiccups in the past, but now we're on track. I just want to make sure it stays that way,"

"I'm only here to help."

"You just never know who you can trust," I said.

"I understand, but I'm totally loyal. I mean, I'm risking a lot to even consider helping with his operation."

"Yeah, you really are! Coffee would never allow me to take such a risk. But, he must know that you're up to it."

Tiffany looked a little uncomfortable.

"What do you mean?" She asked looking concerned.

"I know Coffee must really think a lot of you, if he's planning to involve you in his work, is all."

"I think a lot of him too," Tiffany said with a smile.

"I know that we've only been dating for a few months but..."

"Mami, my hands got sticky," Tati interrupted, licking her ice cream from her fingers.

"Can you excuse me?" I said taking Tati to the restroom and washing her hands and face with a wet paper towel.

"Mami, is she your friend?" Tati asked.

"She's my coworker," I corrected, leading Tati back to the table.

"Okay where were we?" I asked with a fake smile.

"I'm not sure," Tiffany said returning the smile.

"Well, I just want you to know that I trust Coffee's judgment, so if he trusts you, so do I."

"Thanks, Madam Mi. That means a lot. I was hoping we could be friends," Tiffany said naïvely.

I shot Tati a look before she could say anything.

"Sure," I agreed with a smile.

"So how did you and Coffee meet?"

"I was on campus studying, and he walked over and offered to buy me a drink," Tiffany smiled at the thought.

"He's a gentleman," I said forcing a smile.

"It was the funniest thing. We were in a coffee shop, so when he told me his name I just knew he was joking," Tiffany laughed.

"What a coincidence."

"Yeah, so after a latte and a long conversation, we exchanged numbers. I guess the rest is history," Tiffany concluded with a smile.

"I wonder why he was on the college campus. Coffee isn't enrolled in school. Maybe he was looking for girls," I said nonchalantly.

"What do you mean?" Tiffany's smile faded.

"You know, girls to expand the business," I said casually.

"It was good chatting with you, Tiffany. I'm glad we were able to clear the air, but I have to get going." I got up from the table.

"Sure, I have a class in a few hours anyway. It was nice talking to you, Madam Mi," Tiffany said getting up and giving me a quick hug.

"Bye Tati," she said before rushing towards the parking lot to her car.

I text Coffee and told him I had a chat with Tiffany, and I decided to give her a chance.

That night, I was lounging around the house in sweatpants and a t-shirt, watching movies with Tati when Justine called. I told her to come over. She'd just gotten off work and was on her way to get something to eat. She showed up twenty minutes later with cartons of Chinese food. Tati followed me downstairs to let her in.

"Hey, Tati," Justine said handing me the food.

"Hi, Jess. You wanna watch a movie with us?"

"Sure, are you hungry?"

"Nope, I got gummy worms," Tati said excitedly.

"Well, aren't you the coolest legal guardian ever," Justine teased, looking at me.

"It's Friday night and not like she has school in the morning."

"Whatever you say, Mama Mi," Justine joked, as we headed upstairs to my room.

"So, what's been going on with you?" I asked as soon as we'd gotten settled on my king-size bed with our food.

"Guess what I heard at the shop today?" Justine asked in full gossip mode.

"What?"

"My client's cousin is friends with Rick's little sister, and she told her that Rick is back with Kim!"

"Who the hell is Kim?"

"His baby mama."

"Oh well, it's a good thing you got a good source," I said sarcastically.

"Girl, it doesn't matter who the source is, if the information is true."

"So, you're still feeling Rick?" I asked accusingly.

"No, but he's been texting me ever since we ran into each other at Marlene's birthday party."

"Really? Wasn't that a few months back?"

"Yup, but now I find out he's still checking for his baby mama, and I'm just over it!"

I rolled my eyes.

"Jess, you know you're my girl, but you are so sprung on

Rick! I don't think you will ever get over him," I said matter of fact like as I ate my chow mein noodles.

"Oh please, the dick wasn't even good," Justine said rolling her eyes.

"Jess!" I said nodding towards Tati, who was sitting on the floor watching her movie while stuffing her mouth with handfuls of popcorn and candy.

"Oh, sorry," Justine said lowering her voice.

"But that's my point exactly. He's not bringing much to the table, but you still be checking for him. So I know it's love," I teased.

Justine laughed.

"So, what about you? Will you ever settle down, or is pimping just your nature?" Justine asked with a laugh, but then said, "I didn't mean to offend you," when she noticed I wasn't laughing.

"Girl I'm not offended. I'm just thinking about my own men problems."

Justine's green eyes grew wide with curiosity.

"What? You having men problems? That's hard to believe."

I laughed at her astonishment, as my cell phone began to ring. It was Coffee.

"I gotta take this, it's business," I said grabbing my phone and walking outside to the balcony.

I closed the door behind me.

"Hello."

"Mia, what are you up to?"

"Oh nothing, just chilling. What's up?" I asked enjoying the cold night breeze.

"No, I mean what are you plotting? Why would you meet

up with Tiffany, and put all these crazy ideas in her head?" he asked accusingly.

"What are you talking about?" I asked innocently with a smile on my face.

"Mia, don't play dumb. You know what I'm talking about, and you know you don't like Tiffany, so what game are you playing?"

I wanted to tell Coffee that I wanted him back and that Tiffany would never understand him the way that I did. I'd left him because I was hurt and felt betrayed, but I could never love another man the way I loved him. I wanted to tell Coffee that we belonged together.

Instead I said, "I was being the bigger person by meeting up with her and accepting her as a business partner. If you can't control your girlfriends insecurities, that's your problem."

I hung up.

Twenty-One

"I don't care what you say, Destiny, I still think Brandy was crazy to even have that baby," Miracle said talking loudly on her cell phone to her twin sister.

"Meal ticket? Yeah right. She'll be lucky if she get diapers. It's just not realistic to have your pimp's baby and live happily ever after," she laughed.

"Okay, I gotta go." The other girls began to come into the makeup room.

"What's going on?" Blondie asked sitting at her vanity table wrapped in her bath towel.

"My sister says Brandy got the DNA test results back and rumor is, the baby is Coffee's!" Miracle gossiped.

"Shut up! What are the odds of that?" Blondie asked surprised.

"Are they sure?" Lexi asked.

"Yeah, girl, 99.9999% sure!" Miracle said with a laugh.

"That Chica is gonna be paid!" Erica said excitedly.

"I doubt Coffee will give her a dime," Miracle said shaking her head.

"He gonna have to, Chica. It's called child support," Erica argued.

"It ain't like Coffee's money is legal. No way the government can take a cut when they don't know about it," Miracle explained.

"All she has to do is get a good lawyer," Lexi said knowingly, brushing her long blonde hair.

The other girls cracked up laughing.

"She might as well go pick out her own coffin while she's ahead," Trish said in her southern accent.

"That girl may be a lot of things, but Brandy is not crazy. She knows better than to snitch on Coffee," Miracle said knowingly.

"Whose business are y'all talking about today?" Layla asked as she entered the makeup room.

"Just this girl that was dumb enough to have a baby by her pimp," Blondie gossiped.

"This Chica used to live here, but her ass got kicked out when Madam Mi found out about it," Erica added.

"I don't think she's gonna keep the baby. Destiny said she's all cracked out now and she's planning to leave the baby on a doorstep and go back to Ohio," Miracle said.

"That's so sad, another baby in the system," Trish said solemnly.

"I don't see how a mother could ever leave her child. I take care of mines," Layla bragged.

"You got kids, Chica?" Erica pried.

"Yeah, and they are all well provided for," Layla said defensively.

"I would never mess up my body with a baby," Blondie said as she did her makeup.

Layla rolled her eyes.

"I want kids one day," Trish confessed.

"Little Tati is just so cute."

"You can't have a black baby," Blondie said.

"What's that supposed to mean?" Layla asked annoyed.

"Trish is white, so her baby won't look like Tati," Blondie explained with a shrug.

"Well, Brandy is white, and I heard her baby look just like Coffee," Miracle said.

The girls gasped as they noticed I was standing in the doorway.

"Hurry up. Your rides are downstairs," I informed them before turning and going back to my bedroom.

I was becoming annoyed with Miracles constant need to gossip. I'd decided if she continued to talk about other people's business, I would kick her out just like I'd done her big mouth sister.

I hadn't spoken to Coffee since our phone conversation on my balcony. I knew he was upset with me, but I hoped I had created enough doubt in Tiffany's head for her to back out of the business and ultimately end their relationship. She was easy to manipulate, so it was only a matter of time before her insecurities ate away at her peace of mind. If there was one thing I were sure of when it came to Coffee, he did not like to be questioned. I decided to call Tiffany to see where they stood.

"Hey, Tiff. I'm going shopping in the morning. Just wondering if you wanted to join me?"

Tiffany hesitated.

"Are you sure?" She asked sounding skeptical.

"Yeah, why not? It'll be fun," I persuaded.

"Coffee doesn't think it's a good idea for us to be friends."

"Really? I thought he'd be happy to see us getting along," I said sounding disappointed.

"I don't know, Madam Mi, I don't want any drama," Tiffany said as though she had been brainwashed.

"Trust me, I understand. I'm sure you and Coffee have had enough drama, with the new baby and all," I said casually.

"What baby?" Tiffany asked puzzled.

I smiled.

"Coffee didn't tell you?" I pretended to be surprised.

"Madam Mi, what are you talking about?" Tiffany asked sounding concerned.

"I shouldn't have said anything. I didn't know you didn't know about his child. I'm sorry I brought it up. I have to go," I said rushing off the phone.

"Wait!" Tiffany said before I could hang up.

"What time are you going shopping tomorrow?"

"I'll be at the mall tomorrow around ten."

"Okay, I'll see you there," Tiffany said before hanging up.

As I began to drift off to sleep, my cell phone rang. At first I was surprised to see that it was Coffee, but then I figured Tiffany had confronted him and he was calling to curse me out.

"Mia, are you awake?" Coffee asked in his deep, raspy voice.

"Yeah what's up?" I asked sitting up.

"I'm outside. Come open the door."

"Okay, I'll be right there," I ran downstairs wearing only a t-shirt and panties.

When I opened the front door, Coffee was standing there holding a car seat.

I was shocked as Coffee came inside, and I looked at the small baby bundled up in blue blankets.

"This is my son."

"What?"

I peered in at the small light-skinned baby with Coffee's facial features. The baby began to wake up and cry.

"Mia, I need your help," Coffee sounding panicked.

"Brandy dropped him off at my granny's house and just took off. She's not interested in being a mother."

I unbuckled the car seat straps and picked the baby up, rubbing his back to soothe him back to sleep.

"Coffee, where is his bottle and diaper bag?"

"She didn't bring one."

"No diapers?" I asked surprised.

"No, this is how she dropped him off."

"Okay, you have to go to the 24 hour convenience store up the street and get him a bottle, formula, diapers and baby wipes. That should get him through the night. You can get him everything else in the morning," I said, still rubbing his back.

"Alright, but why don't you come with me?"

"No, I'll stay here with the baby. Tati is upstairs asleep," I whispered so I wouldn't wake the now sleeping baby.

"Okay, I'll be right back," Coffee said as he headed to the front door.

"Coffee, what's his name?"

"C.J."

I carried C.J. upstairs to my bedroom and rocked him. When Coffee came back he was asleep in my bed.

Coffee sat beside me and watched C.J. as he slept for a few minutes without saying anything.

"Are you sure he's yours?" I asked, already knowing the answer.

"Yeah, he's mine."

"What are you going to do?"

Coffee shrugged.

"He's my son. I have to take care of him."

"Have you told Tiffany?"

"No, not yet."

"Why did you come here?" I asked curiously.

"I was just hoping you would help me. I don't know the first thing about a baby."

"Except how to make one," I said bitterly.

"I'm sorry I hurt you, Mia, but I can't apologize for my son. He is a part of me. I didn't plan for him, but I love him." Coffee said, watching C.J. sleep.

"I can understand that."

"You can both stay the night, but tomorrow I think you should talk to Tiffany."

"I don't think Tiffany and I are going to work out."

"Because of C.J.?"

"No, we've been having problems and she doesn't even know about C.J."

"She knows."

"What do you mean?" Coffee asked confused.

"When I talked to her earlier it kind of slipped out that you had a baby."

"How could that slip out?"

"Okay, I mentioned it on purpose."

"Why would you do that Mia?" Coffee asked angrily.

"Because I figured if she knew, she would probably leave you and I needed her out of the picture," I said shamelessly.

Coffee stood up looking at me, astounded.

"I'm sorry I tried to sabotage your relationship, but I won't apologize if it's over," I said coldly.

"Mia, I feel like I don't even know who you are!"

"Coffee, I wanted you back and your relationship with Tiffany was preventing us from being together. I just wanted us to go back to the way we were before. I'm still in love with you," I confessed.

"Mia, I love you too," Coffee said leaning in to kiss me.

C.J. woke up and began to cry before our lips could touch.

Twenty-Two

Having a full house took some time to get used to, but after a few months we were adjusting. Every room in the house was occupied and my seven-bedroom home suddenly felt small. The guestroom was changed into C.J.'s nursery, but he ended up spending most of his time in our master bedroom. When C.J. arrived without so much as a baby bottle, he was only two months old. He was now eight months old, and I was the only Mama he could remember. C.J. was a happy, smiling, chubby-cheeked baby. He was my baby! I'd grown so attached to him.

Even with Annabelle's help during the day, I was the one who usually took care of him. I stayed up many nights bouncing and rocking him as he cooed up at me, staring at my face with his big brown eyes. There were times when even Coffee couldn't get him quiet, and he would become frustrated with C.J.'s constant crying. When Coffee handed him over to me, C.J. would nestle up in the crook of my neck and drift peacefully off to sleep. Coffee said I was a natural, as he watched me care for C.J. When he'd first come to live with us, I had to show Coffee how to change his diaper, and although he often used too many baby wipes, he'd gotten it down.

C.J. had recently learned how to crawl, and he wanted to

follow Tati around the house. He'd fuss when she didn't wait for him to catch up. Tati mostly adored C.J. She'd play with him and kiss his chubby-cheeks, but there were other times when she just wanted to do her own thing.

She'd complain that C.J. had destroyed something or another that she'd left unattended.

Since we'd gotten back together, Coffee and I had grown closer than we'd ever been. We were a team when it came to raising the kids, partners in business as well as lovers. I was happy.

There was no indication that there was a problem until Coffee came home one evening and was noticeably upset. He went straight upstairs and slammed our bedroom door.

Annabelle was helping Tati with her homework at the kitchen table, and I'd just laid C.J. down for a late nap. When I went into our bedroom, I saw Coffee outside on the balcony using his cell phone. I could tell from his mannerisms that he was arguing with whoever was on the other end of the phone. I sat at the foot of our bed and waited for him to come back inside.

"Hey Mia," Coffee said trying to sound casual, as he came inside closing the sliding door.

"What's wrong?"

"I'm going to go take a shower," Coffee said walking passed me and going into the bathroom.

When I heard the shower water come on, I took Coffee's phone off the dresser with hopes of getting to the bottom of what had gotten him so upset. To my dismay, the screen was locked and I didn't know his password. I would have to just get the information from Coffee when he was ready to share it with me. When he got out of the shower smelling good with a towel wrapped around his waist, I couldn't resist draping my arms over his shoulders and kissing him, hoping to melt his worries away. Coffee kissed me back, but he seemed so distracted.

"Mia, I gotta get dressed. There's something I gotta take care of."

I knew I wouldn't get anywhere if I attempted to pry into his business for details, so I decided I would focus on my end of the business and allow him to come to me when he was ready.

My business was doing well. The working girls no longer had access to the pool house because Tati was getting older, and I didn't want her exposed to what was going on. She'd overheard the girls talking once, and she'd asked me why all their boyfriends were named John. After that, I decided to make some changes. Coffee had expanded our businesses into new territory which had almost doubled our income, but with his new business ventures came more problems. Coffee was still well known and respected. He was young and powerful, so many of the older men in the business saw him as a threat and viewed his success with envious, jealous eyes.

The more Coffee beefed up his security, the more I feared for his safety. If he saw someone as a threat to his business on Monday, there would be no mention of what happened to them by Wednesday. I knew Coffee was taking risks, although he would assure me that he had everything under control. I'd learned to stop asking for details and just go along with things.

Coffee didn't come home that night until two in the

morning. When I heard his key in the lock, I went to the top of the stairs and saw that he and a few members from his staff were standing by the front door, talking in hushed voices.

"I don't care who he is. Stone may have just gotten out, but this is my turf now, and I'm not backing out of my territory for nobody!" Coffee said raising his voice.

"Boss, Stone is a one-man army because his crew is still locked up," I heard Rick say.

"So, we will take care of Stone now and deal with his men when the time arises," Coffee decided.

I tiptoed back inside our room and climbed back into bed so I wouldn't be caught eavesdropping.

Over the next few days, Coffee went from stressed to relaxed, so I knew that whatever the problem was, it had been taken care of. Coffee acknowledged he hadn't had much time for me lately, and he'd planned a weekend getaway for just the two of us. At first I was reluctant to leave the kids, but Coffee's granny convinced me she had it under control. Tati was excited to go with Granny for the weekend and promised she'd help her take care of C.J. A weekend getaway was exactly what we needed.

While we were away, we didn't leave the room almost the entire time. I enjoyed sleeping in and waking up in Coffee's arms. We ordered room service for nearly every meal and took advantage of the king-size bed that we didn't have to share with C.J.

On our last night of our vacation, we went out to dinner. I was glad Coffee had convinced me to go, because I'd started to opt for another night in. He'd made reservations at a five-star restaurant and was excited to take me out. I complied and put on a short, red, sexy dress paired with ankle-strapped black stilettos. I wore my hair jet black with a straight center part and 22" hair extensions.

Coffee stood smiling in the doorway of the bathroom, watching me apply my makeup.

"What?" I asked when I noticed him looking me over.

"You're so beautiful," he complimented me.

"If you keep flirting with me, we're going to miss dinner," I smiled.

"Let's go, before I take you up on your offer."

He took me by my wrist and rushed me out of the room.

I grabbed my purse on the way out. Dinner was delicious and as I sat across from Coffee drinking white wine, I was surprised when we were joined by a violinist. He appeared next to our table and began to play for us. It was very romantic and thoughtful of Coffee to plan such a romantic evening.

When the piece was over, I clapped and was taken aback by Coffee standing up and then taking a knee in front of me, holding a small, velvet black box. My heart began to beat fast, as he opened the box displaying a big, beautiful, diamond ring.

"Mia Nicole Sampson, you are a beautiful person, inside and out. You're the love of my life and a wonderful mother. Will you do me the honor of being my wife?"

I nodded as tears of joy rolled down my face.

"Mia, will you marry me?" Coffee asked as I gave him my hand.

"Yes," I managed to say.

The restaurant erupted into applause and I realized we were the center of attention. As I looked around, I noticed our friends and family were there scattered amongst the restaurant's staff and customers. I was surprised, as Mama rushed over to me and gave me a hug.

"Congratulations baby," she said, followed by Justine, Shelly, Granny, Natalie and Tori.

Everyone was congratulating us and gushing over my new bling. I was overwhelmed with emotion.

Twenty-Three

Almost as soon as we got back home, I started planning for our wedding. I was excited to be getting married, but I told Coffee I would settle for a small ceremony or even an elopement. He was set on a big, over-the-top wedding. I figured he might have high expectations of what a wedding should be like, when I remembered how extravagant his mother and Tori's ceremony was in Las Vegas. I'd never dreamt of an extravagant wedding, and since my daddy wouldn't be able to walk me down the aisle, I would have preferred to just keep it simple. But, this was Coffee's wedding too.

Justine begged to go dress shopping with me and between her and Mama, I had over a dozen different bridal dress ideas. It was all so overwhelming, but exciting.

"What do you think about pink and grey for our wedding colors?" I asked Coffee as I flipped through the pages of a bridal magazine.

"Yeah, whatever you want," he answered as he text on his cell phone, distracted.

"What if I wore nothing," I suggested, knowing that Coffee wasn't paying attention.

"Yeah, sounds good."

"Babe, if we're going to have a big wedding, I need you to help me plan it," feeling frustrated at the lack of attention Coffee was giving me.

"Alright, Babe, you just gotta give me a second, I'm taking care of some business," Coffee explained without looking up from his cell phone.

Before I could respond, C.J. began to cry from his crib. When C.J. saw me enter his nursery, he held onto his crib rails and pulled himself up.

"Ba ba," C.J. said waving his empty bottle.

I picked him up and headed downstairs to refill his bottle when I noticed the girls were in the makeup room, getting ready for the night.

"Madam Mi, Rick said he's dropping us off early because he has some business to tend to later," Lexi said applying her red lipstick.

I stood in the doorway holding C.J. on my hip.

"That's fine. Come on Tati, you need to get ready for bed," I said as I watched Tati stare at her reflection in the vanity mirror.

"Mami, Trish said I have pretty hair. Can I wear my hair down like hers?"

"Sure, but it's time for bed. You can get your hair straightened tomorrow."

"Ahhh man," Tati whined as she got up from her seat.

"Goodnight, Chica," Erica said to Tati as she looked herself over in the full-length mirror.

She wore a short, red, strapless dress that was tight and clung to her curves. I turned to walk away from the doorway when I heard three loud gunshots.

"Pop! Pop! Pop!" The glass windows downstairs began to shatter with every gun shot fired. Things seemed to be happening in slow motion. I saw the girls frantically rush for cover and I could hear their instant screaming, but I was frozen as the reality of what was happening began to set in.

Coffee ran out of our bedroom and down the stairs holding his gun.

"Mia! Get down!" he ordered before he disappeared out the front door.

Our house was being riddled with bullets. The sounds of the breaking glass and gunshots echoed in my ears.

My instincts pulled me from my shock, I held C.J. close to my chest and I moved quickly, grabbing Tati by her waist and crouching underneath the vanity table. Tati was covering her ears and screaming at the top of her lungs, as I tried to console her. My heart was racing from fear as the bullet spree continued for the next few minutes. When they stopped, there were only the sounds of crying and whimpering from inside the room.

I hesitated to come from underneath the table until I heard the front door open and then slam shut. I put C.J. down next to Tati.

"Stay here," I ordered before crawling out and running to the top of the stairs.

Coffee stood in the foyer with the front of his shirt covered in blood, as he supported Rick's weight with the help of Tony.

"Mia, call an ambulance!" he demanded.

I stood there feeling relief and shock, as I realized the

blood on Coffee's clothes was not his own. Rick's blood was spilling from his weightless body onto the hardwood floors.

"Mia! Now!" Coffee yelled.

I was pulled out of my daze and rushed towards our bedroom to get my cell phone.

Before I got there, I heard a loud piercing scream come from the makeup room.

"She's dead!" I heard Blondie cry out.

"Oh, my god! She's dead!" She yelled frantically.

I ran back into the makeup room and saw Erica's lifeless body on the floor in a puddle of her own blood.

She'd been shot in the chest and her red dress was wet and blood stained. I grabbed C.J. and Tati and put them inside my bedroom as I dialed 9-1-1 with the sounds of the girls screaming and crying in the background.

Erica Lizette Jimenez was laid to rest at Sunset Cemetery three weeks later. A stray bullet had entered my home through the second story window, piercing her chest cavity and tragically taking her life. She had a small, short funeral service with a total of six family members in attendance who came to pay their respects and mourn her death.

None of the working girls attended her service. I saw the police officers that were assigned to investigate the case patrolling the area, as though someone was going to offer them some information.

I'd paid for her funeral arrangements, but did not go inside for the service. I sat in a cab as I looked through the tinted windows behind my dark sunshades. I sat across the street from the cemetery. I said a prayer and asked God to rest her soul and told the driver to take me home. We were staying at Coffee's granny's house until ours could be repaired. Most of the windows had been shot out and there were bullet holes in the garage door and in the stucco outside the house. Downstairs the wood floors were stained with blood from Rick's gunshot wound, and upstairs was still taped off with yellow tape. It was considered a crime scene. The investigation was still ongoing.

The doctors said Rick was lucky to be alive. He'd lost so much blood from the gunshot wound to his stomach, that for a while they weren't sure if he'd make it. After two blood transfusions, Rick pulled through, but he was still being hospitalized because of the extent of his injuries.

The doctor predicted that Rick would never be able to walk again.

Twenty-Four

After the night of the shooting, everything changed. My life as I knew it would never be the same. The shooting was turf retaliation, coordinated by one of the most respected players in the game. He believed Coffee had disrespected his territory, and he'd sent his men to our house that night to take his life. He'd planned to kill Coffee, and to teach a lesson to those who hadn't been loyal while he had been in prison. He'd been the town's major drug lord and pimp until he was locked up. Coffee had taken over his turf, killed half his staff, and stolen his working girls. He held Coffee responsible for ruining the empire he'd built. Now he was free, and he'd come for revenge. He was believed to be ruthless and everyone referred to him as Stone. We lived in a small town, so I knew that he must have heard of me if he knew all about Coffee.

I was the only thing standing in the way of Stone reclaiming what he believed was rightfully his. Coffee had been arrested and booked on a gun charge. Luckily, that was the only thing the police had on him. One of the neighbors gave a statement saying Coffee had been part of the shootout. No one else was talking. So as much as the police wanted to charge Coffee with something that would put him away for good, they had no evidence that he'd been a part of anything more than the shootout. Our lawyers were pleading self-defense. So far, our chances looked good. As long as everyone who knew the details of Coffee's business kept their mouths shut, he would be free in no time. Until then, I was the boss.

I ran both ends of our business, and kept a low profile. I couldn't risk being taken out by Stone. I had to keep business afloat until Coffee could get out and handle everything. I only dealt directly with three of Coffee's men, because I trusted them and I needed a small, secure, circle.

In Sundown Valley, I became more of a figurative character rather than an actual person. That was fine with me, because it had gotten back to me that "The Madam" was merciless and cold blooded when it came to her business. I hid behind my reputation that the town had created for me. It provided protection from any opportunist who knew Coffee was locked up. I kept a 9mm handgun on me at all times, just in case my reputation wasn't enough to protect me. Xavier took me to the shooting range and taught me how to shoot. When I got the gun, I hadn't planned on using it. But it made me feel good that I knew how to shoot, and I wouldn't be scared to defend myself.

To keep a low profile, I had to downsize. I didn't want to attract unnecessary attention to myself. I sold my pink Bentley and used rental cars and cabs to get around. I didn't stay at Granny's house often, because I didn't want to put her and the kids in danger. I figured it was best for me to keep my distance, just in case I were being followed or watched.

I hired Annabelle full-time to help Granny with the kids and I slept in different hotel rooms, trying not to stay anywhere too long. I was determined to not allow Stone or his crew to catch up with me. I was on a mission to free Coffee, preserve our business, and protect our family. I decided if Stone were the threat, he would have to be removed.

I would go see Coffee regularly and keep him updated on the business. He was being held at the county jail and he still didn't have a date for his bail hearing. I was forced to talk to him through a phone receiver as we sat separated by a thick piece of glass. Coffee had made it clear that he wanted me to bring one of his staff members with me during our visits because there were things he couldn't say without jeopardizing his case and his men understood his code words and phrases. Coffee's plan was for me to stay low and out of Dodge until he could handle things, but I had a plan of my own.

While Coffee was locked up, I was running the show. After a call from Tony, I was even more determined to get rid of Stone. He told me that Stone was in the process of reclaiming his turf and he'd intercepted some of the product Coffee's men were transporting. He didn't care about the product; he was just trying to send a message to Coffee's staff that he was taking over. They could get on board or get out of the game, either by choice or force.

Tony informed me that his next move would be to send a similar message to the working girls. He intended on reclaiming his track and reestablishing his reputation as the main pimp in Sundown Valley. I wasn't about to sit back and let Stone just take over everything Coffee and I had worked so hard to establish. I didn't care if he'd lost his operation while he was locked up. That wasn't my problem. I didn't owe him anything. However, since Stone had put a hit out on Coffee, killed Erica, and ruined my home, my vengeance wasn't just business. It was personal.

In order to get rid of Stone, I would have to learn his habits. I needed to stay a step ahead of him. Unfortunately, he was a hard man to find. I could not allow him to steal my product without repercussions. Tony was only able to get the name of one of his men who was part of the drug heist. I put a hit out on him, because I was going to send a message of my own. Stone took my product, so I was going to take one of his men. I didn't care about the details of his execution. I just ordered it to be done as soon as possible and for my product to be left at the scene. I wanted Stone to have no doubt of who ordered the hit. Also, I knew leaving the drugs at the crime scene would make the police write the murder off as a drug related crime, and there wouldn't be much of an investigation. I suspected that the death of his staff would provoke him into payback. The more he responded, the easier it would be for me to track him down.

There would probably be a lot of bloodshed, but I was willing to make the sacrifice in order to smoke him out of whatever hole he was hiding in, and then game over. Of course, it was risky going through with my plan, but I had the advantage, since I was running an empire and he was trying to rebuild one.

"It's done," Tony said through the phone before he hung up.

The next two weeks, I waited anxiously for Stone's retaliation but to no avail. I had underestimated him, and I was growing impatient waiting for his next move. I had a few of my men searching for Stone and his crew, and I was becoming stir crazy hiding out in my hotel room waiting for an update.

Just when I had almost lost hope, I got the call. One of my girls had spotted Stone having an altercation with a white working girl. He must've been her pimp, because after they were seen arguing, she handed him a wad of money and went back to her corner.

"Who is she?" I asked Xavier when we met up at a small café.

"They call her Sandy," he informed me after taking a long sip of his coffee.

"And?"

"She's not on the track often, but the word is she has a history working for Stone and now she's back on his roster."

"She's my girl," I said feeling relieved.

"Madam, don't you think we should consult with the boss before we go through with this plan of yours?" Xavier asked hesitantly.

"Coffee is indisposed. I'm the boss. I'm paying for your services, but if you're not up for the job, I can hire someone who is."

"Madam, I didn't say I couldn't handle the job. I just want to make sure Boss won't have me killed for putting you in a dangerous situation."

"You don't have anything to worry about," I assured him.

"Now that he has been spotted on the track, maybe we should just wait for him to return. We can make the hit without you having to be involved."

"I've waited long enough. I'm going forth with my plan. Set up a meeting for me with Sandy," I ordered.

"Alright," Xavier said with a sigh.

"I'll be in touch," I said as I walked out.

Sandy was strung out from doing so many drugs, that I doubted she would even remember our conversation. I had Xavier pick her up from the track and take her to a cheap motel downtown. I waited in the room for them. She stumbled in high as a kite.

"Oh y'all some freaks huh," Sandy said with a husky laugh when she noticed me sitting on the edge of the bed.

"It ain't that type of party," I said looking at her with disgust.

"I just need to talk to you,"

Sandy looked from me to Xavier looking worried, but before she could respond I took out a wad of money and her glossy eyes grew wide with greed.

"I want to work for your pimp."

"So? You gonna pay me to work for Stone?" Sandy asked puzzled.

"I can't get in touch with him and I want him to add me to his roster. I'm new in town and I don't have no pimp to look after me."

Sandy looked at Xavier,

"So, who the hell is he?"

"He's just a John who said he knew a good whore who could find me a pimp," I said with a shrug.

"So what you want from me?" Sandy asked impatiently.

I handed her the money.

"Get me a meeting with Stone. Tell him I want to be his working girl."

Sandy stuffed the money in her tube top.

"That's it?" she asked.

"Yeah, but I just gave you all my money, so I need you to act fast. I can't work these streets without protection."

"Well, I'll tell Stone you wanna come work for him, but once he put you on his roster, there ain't no going back," Sandy warned.

I nodded my head in understanding.

"He's a real bastard," Sandy said wiping her nose.

"How soon can I meet with him?"

"Stone will be back in town probably tomorrow night," Sandy said sniffing.

"Set up a meeting for me, and I will get you some good product."

"You holding?" Sandy asked excitedly.

"Get me Stone by tomorrow."

"Meet me on the track tomorrow at nine."

Twenty-Five

I didn't have much confidence in Sandy setting up a meeting between me and Stone, but now that she believed I was a working girl, I could use her to get to him. I showed up at the track at nine o'clock with hopes that Stone would come by. If he did, I would be ready for him. I was disguised in a red wig and bright red lipstick. I wore a short, black leather mini skirt and thigh high boots. My handgun was tucked securely in the holster on the inside of my right boot.

I wore a red halter top and a face full of makeup. I wasn't recognizable in my get up. Since Stone didn't know who I was, I wasn't worried about him recognizing me so much as I was that the other working girls might. I had Tony park a few feet away in case I needed backup, but I made it clear that I was the one who was going to take Stone out. I wanted the satisfaction of doing this job myself.

I saw Sandy on the corner fidgeting, trying to light her cigarette. It was cold and windy outside. The wind blew her flame off the lighter before it could burn the end of her cigarette. I cuffed my hands and shielded the wind for her.

"Thanks, Hun," she said in her low hoarse voice.

"I ain't got another one though, I just bummed this one," she said taking a long drag from her cigarette.

"I didn't ask for a smoke. I asked you to setup a meeting with me and Stone," I said trying to jog her memory.

"Oh yeah, I'm working on it," she said looking me over.

"I paid you already! You better work fast," I said raising my voice.

"Look, Hun, I don't want no problems. I'm just trying to do my job," Sandy said defensively putting her hands up and backing away. I took out a small Ziploc bag from my halter top and Sandy's mannerism changed instantly.

"Maybe we can work something out," she said staring at the white substance I dangled in front of her face.

"I want Stone," I said tucking the bag back in my bra.

"Wait a minute, I can get you a meeting with Stone," Sandy begged.

"Tonight," I demanded.

"Chubbz is working for Stone tonight so all you gotta do is talk to Chubbz, and he'll take you to Stone," Sandy suggested fidgeting.

"No, I paid you. You take me to Stone, and then I'll give you the rest of your payment" I referred to the drugs that Sandy was lusting after with her beady eyes.

"Okay, come on."

Sandy was so thin she was practically skin and bones and her high heels made her look like she was walking on stilts.

I followed behind her for two blocks until we reached Third and H St. She led me across the street to an old grey Cadillac that appeared to be empty. As we got closer, I noticed the driver's seat was laid almost completely back and the driver was asleep. Sandy knocked hard on the car window with her pale, white knuckles.

A light skinned fat man sat up and looked annoyed that his sleep was
being interrupted.

"What the hell you want?" he asked as he rolled his window down.

"Hey, Chubbz," Sandy said nervously.

"I'm Mimi, and I want to work for Stone," I interjected getting straight to the point. He looked me over and smirked.

"Is that right?" he asked looking pleased.

I shrugged. "So where is he?"

"I work for him, and I can hire or fire any girl I see fit," Chubbz cut his eye at Sandy.

"No, I'm not gonna go on his roster unless I can meet him personally. No offense, but he has a reputation of being the best pimp in this town, and I want him to know that I work for him."

"Girl, you work for me," Chubbz said aggressively.

"Well, I guess we don't have a deal," I said turning to walk away.

"Mimi, are you new to the track?" Chubbz asked reconsidering my offer.

"Yeah, she's new to town. She just need a pimp," Sandy vouched for me.

Chubbz nodded, looking me over.

"Alright," he agreed.

I felt relieved but I kept my poker face.

"Get in," Chubbz ordered unlocking the backdoor.

"Wait, Hun, don't you got something for me?" Sandy asked grabbing me by my arm.

I pulled away from her.

"Thanks," I said climbing into the backseat.

"Wait you owe me!" Sandy screamed.

"Get back to work," Chubbz said to Sandy and pulled off leaving her standing in the middle of the street.

I knew Tony was probably trailing us from a distance, but regardless, I wasn't scared. I was ready. I was finally going to get rid of Stone and the threat he posed to my family and our businesses. My life could go back to normal once he was gone. I wasn't worried about his staff because I knew they were just on his payroll. With him gone, so was their motive.

We rode in silence for a few minutes and then Chubbz pulled into a small complex of townhomes. When he pulled up and parked, he looked at me in his rearview mirror.

"So, the rule is, I get to sample all the product before we put it on the streets," Chubbz said laughing at his own joke.

I rolled my eyes. I thought about putting a bullet through the back of his head, but I decided I would save my bullets for his boss.

"Girl, I'm just playing with you," Chubbz said with a chuckle.

"Come on," he said getting out of the car.

"Is he here?" I asked, in no mood for his humor.

"Yeah just come in and have a seat," Chubbz ordered.

When we entered the small townhouse, there was music blasting through the stereo. We walked up a flight of green carpeted stairs. The house was dimly lit and smelled like stale cigarette smoke.

A few working girls were at the kitchen table weighting and bagging up product. They were topless and only wore panties. One of the women raised up her bloodshot eyes and looked me over before going back to work.

"Sit down," Chubbz ordered and walked down the hallway and out of sight.

I sat at the edge of a small sofa and avoided the women's eye contact for fear of being recognized. I could feel their nosey eyes looking me over. I strained to make out what was being said in the back room, but the music was too loud and the sounds were muffled.

I waited about fifteen minutes before Chubbz came back, "Come on, let's go," he ordered.

"What?"

"You heard me, let's go!"

"I'm not going anywhere with you. Where is Stone?"

"Look, the boss is in the middle of some important business, and he ain't seeing nobody tonight."

"I ain't going nowhere until I see him," I said standing up and folding my arms.

I heard one of the women at the table laugh and I shot her a dirty look. She looked familiar, but I couldn't quite remember her name.

"I know you're new to town, but you won't last long if you don't know how to take orders."

Just then the music stopped, and I heard footsteps coming from the hallway.

"I don't want a problem, I just need a pimp," I said changing my approach as Chubbz directed his attention towards the hallway.

"Stone, this is the girl I was telling you about," Chubbz explained as a tall figure appeared at the end of the hallway.

As he walked towards me, I slid my hand into my right boot and pulled my gun from the holster. Before Stone could even make eye contact with me I aimed the gun at his face with my finger on the trigger.

"Oh shit!" Chubbz said putting his hands up and backing away. The women in the kitchen screamed and took cover. Stones dark brown eyes met mine and I froze.

"Daddy?!" I exclaimed.

Twenty-Six

"Clear out!" Daddy ordered as Chubbz and the working girls scattered towards the exit.

"Daddy, what are you doing here?" I asked feeling confused.

"Mia, what are you doing?" Daddy asked as he took the gun out of my hand and looked me over.

"Daddy, you're Stone?" I asked in disbelief.

"I'm not sure what you've gotten yourself into, Mia, but I'm not going to allow you to live this way."

Daddy was shaking his head with disappointment in his eyes.

"Daddy I'm not a working girl," I clarified realizing that I was wearing my disguise.

I took off the red wig and attempted to wipe off the red lipstick, feeling embarrassed by my appearance.

"Mia, what are you doing here?" Daddy demanded.

"I didn't know you were Stone, Daddy. When did you get out?" I asked trying to make sense of everything.

"Only a few months ago, and I was going to send for you as soon as I got myself back on my feet."

"I didn't know you were Stone, Daddy. I'm so sorry," I said as my eyes filled with tears.

"I never wanted you to be a part of this business, Mia."

"Daddy, I'm not a working girl! My outfit is only a disguise to get to Stone."

"So why did you come looking for Stone?"

"I came to kill Stone."

Daddy frowned and looked down at the gun he'd taken from my hands.

"I didn't know," I repeated.

"Mia, what are you saying?" Daddy asked confused.

"Daddy, I'm the Madam," I said watching my daddy's eyes widen with disbelief.

"What?"

"Daddy you had your men shoot up my home. You killed one of my working girls. You paralyzed one of my men, and now my fiancée is locked up because he shot back. You had a hit put out on him."

I began to get upset as I remembered the night of the shootout.

"Daddy, I lost everything: my kids, my home, my car, my life. I've been hiding out in hotel rooms. I've even been too afraid to even go visit Mama. You got out of prison and decided you were going to take back a territory that you were no longer entitled to!"

"How did this happen?" Daddy asked becoming angry.

"How in the hell did you get so involved in the business?"

"I've been running my end of the business for years."

"My baby girl is the town's Madam," Daddy said proudly.

"What about this fiancée of yours?

"Where is he?"

"Coffee is still locked up. We're waiting for his bail hearing"

"He put you up to all this?" Daddy asked accusingly.

"No, he doesn't know I planned to take Stone out. I've been running both ends of our business since he's been gone. I gave my men orders to track Sto-...I mean... you down, so I could get rid of the threat to our business and our family."

My Daddy shook his head,

"You jeopardized your life coming here with a gun, Mia. Anything could have happened to you."

"I know, but I had one of my men follow your guy over here. I just wanted to handle this by myself. I knew it was dangerous, but I was determined to do what I felt was necessary to protect my family!"

"Mia, I've missed you so much," Daddy said giving me a hug and kissing me on my forehead.

"I'm sorry that I put you through so much. I had no idea that you had any involvement in the business."

"So where do we go from here?" I asked feeling relieved.

"I suppose I should cancel the hit I have on your head," Daddy said with a laugh, but I knew he wasn't joking.

Once I'd gotten past the shock of my Daddy being released from prison and being the infamous Stone, I was excited to have him back in my life. He told me that Mama wasn't willing to accept him back in hers. She wouldn't even allow him to see Junior. When I was with my Daddy, I often heard them arguing through the telephone.

"That man ain't gonna raise my son, I'm his daddy!"

They'd argue back and forth, but Daddy would always end the conversation saying,

"I love you Rita. Send my love to Junior."

It hurt to see my daddy holding on to the past and knowing Mama had moved on. She had no intentions of ever looking back. Daddy hadn't changed much while he was in prison. He was still short-tempered and violent when it came to the business. He'd given several staff members and working girls black eyes and busted lips when he thought his money was short or that respect was lacking.

Daddy was given the nickname, Stone, because he was thought to be stone hearted and cold. He was in the process of rebuilding his empire. Later, I realized the woman at the table that looked familiar was Daddy's old working girl, Coco. There was no word on what happened to Candy after daddy had been arrested. She was Justine's cousin, but Justine would never mention her, I believe out of embarrassment.

After the shootout, Justine blamed Coffee for what had happened to Rick, so a wedge grew between us. However, after a few years of physical therapy Rick did walk again, with the assistance of a cane. During his recovery, Justine and Rick moved in together and he gave his life over to Christ. When I'd see Justine at the shop or around town, we were cordial, but we weren't close anymore. I understood her loyalty to her man, so I suspected she understood mine.

Coffee was sentenced to six years in prison, and even with the best lawyers he still had to serve the time. I'd finally gotten my father back in my life after ten years of being apart, but I'd lost my fiancée to the same system that had kept my father from me. The business had taken so much from me, yet I could not get out.

My daddy reclaimed his territory and I continued to live life as a Madam. Word had gotten back to Coffee that Stone was my father before I even had a chance to tell him. It seemed as though the whole town was buzzing that the Madam had almost killed her own father over a turf dispute. The Madam had a reputation for being evil and heartless, even more so than her father. There were rumors that I would kill without remorse and there were a lot of fabricated stories to back up this claim. I enjoyed my fictional character because ultimately it kept me and my family safe.

I sold my house and bought a small home for me, Tati, and C.J. I decided I would no longer live with my business for fear of the kids being exposed to the dangers it came with. I knew Tati would never forget what she had witnessed that night of the shooting, and I knew I was personally responsible for not being able to protect her from that situation. Luckily, C.J. was so young at the time that he had no recollection of it. It was a shame that the same couldn't be said about Tati. I wanted to create a life of normalcy for them.

One day as we strolled through the mall, Tati walked alongside me admiring the different outfits the mannequins wore in the window displays. I held C.J. on my hip. I caught a glimpse of our reflection in a store window and it reminded me of when I was young and Daddy had been taken from us. I would trail behind Mama and admire things in the windows that I knew we couldn't afford while Junior was tucked in Mama's arms, the same way I now held on to C.J. For a brief moment our reflection took me back to my childhood. Now that I was an adult in almost the identical situation as my mother, I felt a newfound respect for her that I never had before. Sure, I could afford anything in the stores now, but the realization of my mother working two jobs, and raising two kids by herself made me feel grateful, even though I hadn't always gotten everything I wanted.

Twenty-Seven

"Mami, Tati won't let me go with her," C.J. whined.

"I'll be back. I'm meeting up with Kate at the plaza," Tati said as she put on her jacket.

"Take C.J." I said sorting through my mail in hopes of seeing a letter from Coffee.

"I can't! We're going to the plaza theater and you know he can't sit still through a whole movie," Tati reminded me.

"Can too!" C.J. protested.

"Next time, C.J.," Tati said rushing towards the door.

"Be back by eight," I said as Tati shut the door.

"Mami, that's not fair!" C.J. cried.

Tati had just turned fourteen and she was spending more and more time with her friends and less time at home and with me and C.J. I gave Tati the freedom to go shopping with friends and she'd stay late at school for basketball games without my constant supervision.

She was a good kid and she got good grades. Tati was getting older and this was hard on C.J. because he was getting left behind more.

When I was young, I missed out on a lot, because I was always stuck at home babysitting Junior, and I didn't want to do that to Tati.

"C.J. we can watch a movie here. I'll make popcorn," I offered, attempting to cheer him up.

"No, I wanna watch a movie with Tati," C.J. pouted.

"Fine, I'll just have to eat all the popcorn by myself," I said going into the kitchen.

"Fine then, I'll help you," C.J. said giving in.

C.J was six years old and he looked so much like Coffee, but he had light skin and a head full of curly brown hair. He was so precious to me. I was happy to have a piece of Coffee with me every day.

C.J. didn't remember Coffee outside of jail, but I'd show him pictures and take him with me to visitations. C.J was too young to remember life before Coffee had been arrested.

Coffee had served five of his six year sentence when his case went up for review. He got a date for his early release due to good behavior. I'd waited for Coffee to come home for so long! It had been hard, but we kept in touch for the last five years through weekly letters, pictures, and daily phone calls. I kept money on his books and visited him every Tuesday. When he called, and told me the day he would be released, I bawled like a baby. I felt a weight lifted from me. When Coffee had been taken from me, my life had been put on hold. Although it was Coffee who had been locked up, when he was freed so was I. I was now free to live my happily ever after.

We got married the following summer in an outdoor, Greek Goddess theme ceremony. I wore a short, white toga style wedding dress and gold jewelry. My hair was curled and swept up into an updo and pinned.

I walked down the stone clad aisle barefoot with a gold anklet on and a bouquet of white roses. Our wedding planner had paid attention to every detail and the end result was beautiful. I felt like a goddess walking through the garden. I was escorted down the aisle by my daddy. He nodded his approval to Coffee as I left his arm and took Coffee's hand. Mama sat in the front row smiling with Junior and James. Tati was my bridesmaid and C.J. was Coffee's best man.

As we were pronounced husband and wife, we held hands and jumped together over the wooden broom laid before our feet and entered into a new chapter of our lives.

About the Author

Manassah grew up in the High Desert of Southern California. She was the middle child of 11 children. Despite her unique upbringing, she credits her ability to capture the reader's attention to being relatable and having a vivid imagination.

She is passionate about reading and writing. Manassah enjoys the writing process and finds it to be therapeutic and freeing. Awaiting Honesty was written while she was on bedrest due to having a high-risk pregnancy with her daughter.

Manassah currently lives an ordinary family life. Aside from being an author, she is a wife, mother, and registered nurse.